Praise for *Brides in the Sky:*

"Every tale in this superb collection bursts with distinctive life, and yet all feel eerily connected. Holladay moves with such ease in and out of time, in and out of such a diversity of hearts, that you feel you're under the spell of a guide who knows the secrets of all the old houses on the street. She can show you every room—and the exquisite ghosts therein. Her tour is brilliantly imagined, deeply felt, and beautifully told."

—Tim Johnston, author of *Descent*

"From the Sundance Kid's sweetheart to a child-snatching sorority sister to a heroic telephone operator and more, *Brides in the Sky* exposes the limitations of our assumptions, while deftly reinventing story form. Each narrative here proves an astonishment, a marvel."

—Lorraine M. López, author of *The Darling*

"*Brides in the Sky* is a masterful sweep of time and imagination, and an exceptional display of voice and character. These stories span centuries, livelihoods, and the great dimension of Holladay's impressive creativity and heart. Each story works to pull you into its 'embrace as warm as a rug.' And while you're snuggled there, you look up to the Milky Way's 'great folds and curtains and cobwebs of stars.' *Brides in the Sky* sparkles like these stars."

—Jim Minick, author of *Fire Is Your Water*

Praise for Cary Holladay:

"Good fiction shows us the inside of things—a community, a job, a relationship, the human heart. Great fiction can sometimes show all of these things working together; it lifts us briefly above the event horizon of our own day-to-day existences and gives us a dreamlike (and godlike) sense of understanding what life itself is about. Cary Holladay's 'Merry-Go-Sorry' is one of those rare and always welcome stories."

—Stephen King

BRIDES IN THE SKY

BRIDES

STORIES AND

IN THE

A NOVELLA

SKY

CARY HOLLADAY

Swallow Press / Ohio University Press ✦ Athens

Swallow Press
An imprint of Ohio University Press, Athens, Ohio 45701
ohioswallow.com

Printed in the United States of America
Swallow Press / Ohio University Press books are printed on acid-free paper ⊗ ™

29 28 27 26 25 24 23 22 21 20 19   5 4 3 2 1

The stories below have been previously published in slightly different form.
"Brides in the Sky" and "Operator," *The Hudson Review*
"Shades," *Epoch*
"Comanche Queen," *The Cincinnati Review*
"Interview with Etta Place, Sweetheart of the Sundance Kid," *Freight Stories*
"Ghost Walk," *Philadelphia Noir*
"Hay Season," *Great Jones Street*
Portions of "A Thousand Stings" have been published as stand-alone stories:
"A Thousand Stings," *Shenandoah*; "Summer of Love," *Epoch*; and "The Best Party
Ever," *Oxford American*. "A Thousand Stings" received the Goodheart Prize for Fiction,
awarded by *Shenandoah*.

Although several real-life figures appear in these stories—including Cynthia Ann
Parker, her family members, and the Texas Rangers Sullivan Ross and Tom Kelliher in
"Comanche Queen," and Etta Place and Harry Longabaugh in "Interview with Etta
Place, Sweetheart of the Sundance Kid"—their portrayals are entirely fictitious. All of
the characters, events, and situations in these stories are the product of the author's
imagination.

Library of Congress Cataloging-in-Publication Data
Names: Holladay, Cary C., date. author.
Title: Brides in the sky : stories and a novella / Cary Holladay.
Description: Athens : Swallow Press, 2019.
Identifiers: LCCN 2018043052| ISBN 9780804012034 (hardback) | ISBN
   9780804012041 (pb) | ISBN 9780804040938 (pdf)
Subjects: | BISAC: FICTION / Short Stories (single author). | FICTION /
   General.
Classification: LCC PS3558.O347777 A6 2019 | DDC 813/.54--dc23
LC record available at https://lccn.loc.gov/2018043052

In remembrance of my mother

Catharine Gardner Mitchell Holladay

1925–1994

the first writer I knew.

Mama, the bells of your memory were always ringing.

Contents

Brides in the Sky

IN MARCH 1854, KATE and Olivia Christopher lost their parents to illness and inherited the family farm in Augusta County, Virginia. At one time, there were over a hundred acres, but whenever the Christophers needed money, they'd sold land to a neighbor, Mr. Cole. About thirty acres were left, much of it steep and rocky.

They couldn't get the winter out of their lungs, was how Kate thought of her parents' deaths. The shock of losing them left her unable to cry.

In the burying ground, a light snow was falling.

Mr. Cole approached the sisters. He wore a long black coat. Up close, with his round cheeks, he looked younger than Kate had thought he was. A breeze spun his hat away. He ran to retrieve it and smiled at her.

"If you want to sell," he said, "I'll buy."

She'd been afraid he would ask for her hand, or Olivia's. A bereaved woman, whether widow or daughter, could find herself affianced before the earth was spaded over the coffin. She was eighteen, Olivia twenty, and they had no money. Mr. Cole was a widower and wealthy.

"We don't want to sell," she said, and Olivia didn't contradict her.

"What are you going to do now?" asked Mrs. Spruill, an old friend of their mother's.

"We'll work the farm ourselves," Kate said.

"We'll help you," said Mrs. Spruill, but she and her husband had their own farm and five children.

The next morning, Kate hitched a mule to the plow, and she and Olivia took turns tilling the earth. Their father had hired men to help with the planting and harvesting, and the girls and their mother had put up food for the winter. This was so much harder. How could there be so many stones, when the ground had been plowed before? It was as if rocks grew out of the dirt. Over several weeks, Kate and Olivia planted potatoes, onions, cabbage, radishes, and peas. At night, they stripped off their soiled clothes and crawled between icy sheets. There was no time to keep house. They waited until the middle of May, when there was no chance of frost, to plant squash and beans. Corn was last. They counted groups of four kernels into tiny hills of earth and recited the old rhyme: "One for the blackbird, one for the crow, one for the weather, and one to grow."

The harsh, sloping land filled Kate's vision even in her sleep. Would she and Olivia find husbands, or would their family line simply end? The thought saddened her, but she vowed to be grateful for the life she had.

It was a dry spring, and many of the vegetables failed to sprout. Varmints ravaged the radishes and peas.

"I can't bear it," Olivia said.

Kate took their father's gun and managed to shoot a groundhog. She put it in the stewpot and was glad for the meat. Occasionally, in the spring and the sweltering summer, Mr. Spruill came over with his son Billy, who was thirteen, and they helped hoe the weeds. Those days were easier.

Kate tended the beehives her father had established. One day she and Olivia woke to a great buzzing. A dark mass tapped the window-panes. The bees were swarming. The sisters gathered tin pots and spoons and rushed outside, making a racket, hoping the noise would cause the bees to return to the hives. Instead, they flew away.

"No getting them back," Olivia said.

✦ ✦ ✦

THE harvest was scant, with corn so tough only the mule could eat it. Neighbors left a ham and sacks of meal on the porch. At Christmastime, two young men appeared at church—Andrew and Martin Sibley from Henrico County.

"We're heading west," said Martin, with a smile for Kate. "Plenty of free land in Oregon."

"And gold in California," Andrew said.

"Nobody gets rich in a gold rush except the people who sell things," Martin said, and Kate saw that even though he was the younger brother, he had the cooler head, and they'd likely talked about this before. "We'll be better off farming in the Willamette Valley."

Yet Sunday after Sunday, they showed up. They had found work with Mr. Cole, and they promised to help the sisters at planting time. Kate prayed her thanks to God. When Andrew walked Olivia home from church, it was only natural that Martin would fall into step with Kate. When Andrew and Olivia vanished into the brush, Martin drew Kate into his arms.

"Why shouldn't we?" He kissed her.

Later, when the brothers were gone, Kate faced her sister on their porch. Courtship was flattering, and the blue-eyed men were as handsome as princes. Olivia had high cheekbones and dark, winged eyebrows, but Kate was plain as a biscuit, and uneasy.

"He's better-looking than I am," she said. "Is it us they want, or the farm?"

"Who'd want this?" Olivia swept her arm toward their bleak acres.

It was a double wedding. The Sibley brothers fidgeted at the altar as the sisters stepped into church, wearing their best dresses. After the ceremony, neighbors wished them health and long life. Mrs. Spruill had baked a cake, and everyone had a slice, along with blackberry cordial.

That night, Kate led Martin to the room she'd had since childhood. She felt shy, although they'd been together those times in the woods.

"Are you mine?" he said.

His embrace was as warm as a rug. She fell in love with him at that moment.

✦ ✦ ✦

RIGHT away, Andrew started saying, "It's not enough land."

"I like it here," Martin said.

Andrew pulled out maps and reminded Martin about the thousands of acres out west, free for the taking. Kate was terrified by the fate that had befallen white settlers. Everyone knew about Dr. and Mrs. Whitman, missionaries whose Oregon compound was attacked by Cayuses.

"The Cayuses was hung," Andrew said, "and the army'll send out more soldiers."

"I won't go," said Olivia, her face like stone.

One raw spring day, Mr. Cole came over. He stood on the porch in his long black coat and made an offer to the four of them. Kate looked to Olivia, who hesitated.

"You used to talk about going west," he said to the brothers.

"We'll think about it," said Martin.

"We'll take it," said Andrew.

Olivia went into the house and banged the door behind her. Kate's heart beat like wings. This was what change felt like. Mr. Cole counted out money into Andrew's palm. The porch needed paint, and winter snow had warped the railing. Why notice these things now, when the place was passing out of her hands?

"I'll live here," Mr. Cole said. "I like it better than my house. Will you leave the beehives, Kate?"

She read his solemn eyes and straight mouth. If she'd waited, he'd have asked her to marry him. The realization filled her with regret. It would have been all right. At her parents' funeral, she'd been afraid he would ask, when she should have been encouraging him. She should have gone to him the day the bees swarmed.

"Oh, yes," she said, as she might have replied to a proposal. The passion she was finding in the nights with Martin—would she have found it with Mr. Cole? Maybe not, but still there'd have been children, and she wouldn't have had to leave.

"We can't take beehives in the wagons anyway," Martin said. He put his arm around her.

"Good luck to all of you." Mr. Cole went down the porch steps.

"Look after the barn cats," Kate said.

He turned with his hand on the railing. "I will."

✦ ✦ ✦

ANDREW and Martin used the money to buy oxen and extra-strong wagons made of cypress, with hickory bows and waterproofed canvas covers.

"It's April. We've got to hurry," Andrew said.

Kate and Olivia bundled clothing into trunks. They packed cooking supplies and food.

"I wish I hadn't married him," Olivia said. She was crying. "Aren't you sorry?"

"No." Kate loved Martin too much to believe the brothers had plotted to get their farm and sell it, but she also believed that in marriage, some sort of bargain was struck. "It'll be fine. We'll all be together."

+ + +

THE Spruills went with them, the farmer and his wife and their five children, Hannah, Billy, George, Constance, and Ella. At the last minute, a taciturn carpenter named Zachary Willis joined the group. By the time they reached St. Joseph, Missouri, Kate felt they had traveled as far as the moon. St. Joseph teemed with emigrants. Most were from Illinois, Ohio, and Arkansas, but they came from all over, even England, Ireland, and Scandinavia.

A young couple from Kentucky, James and Susan Edmiston, asked to travel with them. The Edmistons were headed to northern California, and they would take the Oregon Trail until it divided into two main routes. Susan was beautiful, and Kate felt a dart of envy. James Edmiston had a banjo, and Kate was glad there'd be music.

The first company to set out for the Oregon Trail, back in 1843, had consisted of a thousand people. Now that the trails were well worn, groups of any size could go. Theirs was only four wagons, each hauled by four oxen, with a spare pair of oxen, a few horses and mules, and a cow.

They caught up with others as they traveled, and Kate loved swapping treats. For the first time, she ate pickled cauliflower, duck sausage, and Swedish almond cookies. There was talk of President Pierce and slavery. Everyone expected there'd be a war back East. There'd been very few blacks in Augusta County. Kate didn't think slavery would long be a part of the world, nor should be.

The first time she saw an Indian, dark-skinned in leather breeches, her throat closed in fear, but her curiosity was stronger. He knew a little English, and the others they encountered—Arapaho, Crow, Pawnee, and Assiniboine—only wanted food and tobacco. Scarred by smallpox, they hung around campsites. Mrs. Spruill doled out bread and glass jars, which they prized.

Occasionally the party met a go-back.

"I'm wore out," the person might say. "I miss my home folks. You'll go back, too."

Some emigrants pulled or pushed carts themselves, tugging or trundling their loads and crossing the continent on their own two legs. This was the "Foot and Walker Company." Kate was amazed.

She was sore all over from the jouncing wagon, but she loved fording rivers. In Kansas, the Little Blue was shallow but had a quicksand bottom. She held her breath as the water reached the center of the wheels. Moments later, the wagons rolled up on the banks.

Except for Susan Edmiston, who was pregnant, monthlies were a misery the women endured as best they could. Kate and Martin rarely talked about bodily processes. She didn't know many words for them, and he didn't either, except for the vulgar, childish ones. When would she start having babies? She'd heard of an old trick: put a wedding ring up inside. But she didn't, afraid it would hurt a baby or herself.

By unspoken assent, the leader of their company was James Edmiston, lithe, a little arrogant, with a prowling stride made for walking west. He could make everybody laugh, even the silent Zachary Willis. James had a way of holding Kate's gaze while his eyes crinkled and he waited for her to laugh. Martin was quiet and thoughtful, given to chewing his lip. She couldn't help comparing them.

Susan Edmiston had long red hair that Olivia and fifteen-year-old Hannah Spruill took turns combing. Her pregnancy made it thicker.

"She already lost two babies," Olivia told Kate. "James won't leave her alone. She asked me to help her."

Kate felt some darkness fall, and it had nothing to do with the night. The men were playing cards and smoking by the fire. Sunset lit the sky like a red bowl over the prairie.

"Help her how?" asked Kate.

Back home, Olivia would have answered right away, and the answer would have been, *Sew baby clothes. Help her lift the pots.* But she didn't say anything, and Kate felt oddly reluctant to press her.

A clear night came on. The Milky Way bristled across the oceanic darkness.

"There's heaven," said Ella, the youngest Spruill child.

More stars blossomed as they watched, great folds and curtains and cobwebs of stars. Everyone picked out constellations: the Big Dipper, the Herdsman, Berenice's Hair, the Dragon, the Twins, and Taurus the Bull.

"See that cluster of stars on the bull's shoulder?" asked James Edmiston. "It's the Pleiades. The Seven Sisters."

The name charmed Kate. She did a quick tally: herself, Olivia, Susan Edmiston, Mrs. Spruill, and the Spruill daughters, Hannah, Constance, and Ella.

"That's us," she said.

After that, she looked for the Pleiades every night. Two of the stars outshone the others. She imagined they were new brides, herself and Olivia.

Was celestial space any more strange and vast and distant than the land they were traveling across and the unknown place where they were heading? What awaited them all? God moved above them, an invisible shepherd, the stars his knowing eyes. The diamond sky brimmed with leviathans—monsters, animals, and giant symbols, a clock, a sextant, a lyre. Kings and queens capered among them. Surely the ancient stories playing out in the heavens foretold what was to come. The stars' courses paralleled that of Kate's party, following the sun. Night after night, the glittering Seven Sisters sailed west, while the mortals crawled below.

✦   ✦   ✦

AGAINST her will, she felt attracted to James. Sometimes he and Olivia were both absent. *She asked me to help her,* Olivia had said, but she couldn't have meant what Kate was thinking. That was absurd: trail madness. Olivia and James would return to the evening campsite from separate directions, James with kindling, Olivia with a pail of water, and they might have, *must have*, Kate corrected herself, been on innocent errands. Olivia set down the pail. James told funny stories. Andrew laughed, and Kate felt a rush of pity for her brother-in-law, who looked so young in his dirty clothes.

James brought out his banjo and sang a ballad about two sisters who loved the same man. The man preferred the younger one and gave her gifts. The older girl led the younger one to a river and pushed her in, and she drowned.

What a horrible song. James crooned on and on. Did he know how Kate felt about him? Was he poking fun at her and Olivia? He finished with a flourish of strumming, turned the banjo over, and showed Kate a fancy design on the back of the fingerboard, a spray of white flowers.

He handed it to her. "It's mother-of-pearl."

He traced the pattern, his hand touching hers. Embarrassed, she gave it back.

"Why not sing something a little more cheerful?" Susan said.

"How about 'The Wayward Boy'?" Andrew said.

James obliged. "Well, I walked the street with a tap to my feet."

Martin and Andrew joined in. Kate knew the song, a bawdy one about a man who met a maiden in a tower, and soon she had many babies. Martin caught her eye and winked, their signal. They stood up, left the others, and found a place away from camp. He put blankets down. A pair of birds flew up into the beech trees. There was just enough light for her to recognize them as thrushes.

He fumbled at her buttons. "I think about it all the time," he said.

"I do too."

"Does everybody?" he asked shyly.

She buried her face in his neck. If anything ever happened to him, she would have to take another man to bed, and fast. She knew it as she clutched his shoulders and panted into his hair.

✦ ✦ ✦

"I'LL plant an orchard," Mrs. Spruill said. She had brought saplings wrapped in burlap. "I hear the Willamette Valley's grand for fruit trees."

The men took turns riding ahead and staying back, seeing that the women and the wagons were all right. When a horse or mule stumbled, they looked to Mr. Spruill. At fifty, he was the oldest, with a long beard his children liked to play with. They wrapped the ends behind his neck while he pretended to wonder where it had gone.

"Did it take a notion to run away?" He picked at the empty air. "If you see it, will you tell it to come back?"

Fifteen-year-old Hannah just grinned, but the younger children bubbled over with laughter: fourteen-year-old Billy, eleven-year-old George, and Constance and Ella, ages eight and six. Sometimes they walked alongside the wagons, pulling at switches of grass, and everyone's face, even Ella's, was lined and red and hardened from the sun.

On Sunday mornings, they read the Bible, prayed, and sang hymns, sometimes joined by other groups, their harmonious voices rising on the ceaseless grassland wind. The women kept Monday as wash day. They hung the wet garments from the sides of the wagons. The clothing and bedding streamed like pennants and dried fast in the wind. Even when the wash water was muddy, the sun bleached out the white things so they were snowy again.

Thank goodness the Spruills had brought a cow, which gave enough milk for everybody. Leftover milk was placed in covered buckets, and in a day or two, the motion of the wagon churned it to clumps of butter.

"Yankee Doodle went to town, a-riding on a pony," sang the Spruills.

Kate rode ahead with Martin, Andrew, and Zachary. The land rolled out before them in paint-box colors.

A mail carrier approached. "Letters for back East?"

A pang went through Kate. She hadn't written any of her friends or neighbors. Olivia waved a sheaf of letters, and the carrier put them in his leather pouch.

"We've crossed into Nebraska," Martin said.

A bird spun up from the bushes and flaunted long, fluted feathers: a scissor-tailed flycatcher. Kate urged her horse into a trot across the green prairie, for the joy of it.

✦ ✦ ✦

SHE steeled herself for the sight of graves. There were all kinds of markers, from wooden crosses to finely chiseled stone. A packing case protruded from the ground, a makeshift casket that had been unearthed and rifled. The body had been tossed aside, a child's, no longer recognizable as boy or girl, the face eaten away. The men dug a grave and reinterred it.

Kate wished she could climb into her old bed and pull the covers over herself. Virginia would be lush with June showers. Mr. Cole had gotten a great bargain—beehives, barn cats, house, and that lovely, rainy land.

Her tears flowed. If the others saw, let them think she was crying for the reburied child.

✦ ✦ ✦

THE trail was full of death. Emigrants died from fights, lightning strikes, and accidental drowning in rough rivers. They were run over by wheels or kicked by draft animals. Whole parties strayed from the trail and expired from hunger or thirst. Kate averted her eyes from animals' bleached skulls and ribcages.

One day they heard a bell tolling and came upon a funeral. A man was striking the bell with a hammer. Susan gave the mourners a pan of gingerbread. Olivia chided her, and Kate felt it wasn't the gift Olivia begrudged them, but Susan's sympathy.

"Are you all right?" Kate asked Olivia, when they were alone.

Olivia gave a little laugh. "I feel like I forgot something, like I need to go home and get it, but I don't know what it is."

✦ ✦ ✦

"DON'T drink alkali water," warned the seasoned travelers, "and don't let your animals."

For now, there was enough water and game—pronghorn, deer, and sage hens, which were delicious when roasted over the fire.

Sometimes wild mustang ponies thundered past. One morning, a buffalo wandered near camp, shaggy and enormous. Martin aimed his gun but missed, and it shambled away.

"The army wants them all gone," James said, "because that'd get rid of the Indians."

Fifteen, twenty miles a day they covered, yet they needed to move faster. From Missouri, the journey to Oregon or California took at least four months, usually five. It was already July, and winter would come early on the trail.

Kate believed they were charmed. To others came the mishaps and misfortunes—broken axles, capsized ferries, soured potatoes, and bouts of dysentery, typhoid, and measles. People often had themselves to blame for their perils, and illness could strike anywhere. Those who sickened might have done so at home. Her party enjoyed health and well-being.

They bathed in rivers, men and women separately.

"Goodness, my hair's turning white everywhere," Mrs. Spruill said.

"Oh, Ma, don't say that," Hannah said.

Olivia kept charge of the medical supplies. There were clean needles and silk thread to sew torn skin, a bottle of laudanum for pain, sassafras root for catarrh, peppermint for upset stomach. They had pooled their food and bought more, so they had plenty—hams, bacon, apples, onions, potatoes, sweet potatoes, pickles, jam, and dried beans, peas, and pumpkin slices. The Spruill children found Kate's last few jars of honey, packed in straw.

"Let's save that for later," she said. Its scent would make her homesick.

Olivia gave each child a spoonful of molasses instead. Olivia was wise, a sister to be admired. Kate could almost believe the conversation about the Edmistons hadn't happened or she'd misunderstood. She was ashamed of her suspicions.

At night, white-throated sparrows sang in moonlit trees along the rivers, and the Milky Way arched above, magnificent and deeply silent. One night, when the others had gone to bed in the wagons, Kate stayed up, stargazing. Someone brushed her elbow. James.

"In the Greek myths," he said, "Orion chased the Seven Sisters."

"The hunter chased the girls?"

"Yes. They were scared, and they asked Zeus for help."

"And what did he do?"

"He changed them into doves and put them in the sky."

Wolves' howls reached her ears. The eerie, discordant music gave her a reason to move closer to him. If he tried to kiss her, she'd let him.

"It's my turn to keep watch," he said, and was gone.

Day after day, she followed him with her eyes. He could turn her into a bird. He could turn her into anything he wanted to.

✦ ✦ ✦

THE streets of Fort Kearny were full of soldiers. Susan stood up in her wagon, her calico dress straining over her belly, and a dozen hands reached out to help her climb down. What would it be like to be so pretty?

"Don't you think you should stay here until the baby comes?" Kate asked.

"James wants to keep going," Susan said.

Babies were being born all along the trail. Mothers would brandish a newborn and yell out its date of arrival. Other women were sick in the backs of their wagons or dead in childbirth. The trail belonged to men. Wives, daughters, sisters, mothers, and grandmothers were tugged along like the Spruills' cow.

Olivia and Susan posted letters while Kate shopped at the fort's store. At the counter, a woman ducked her head, trying to hide the purple bulges around her eyes.

Why were some beaten and others treated as queens?

Feeling bold, Kate met the soldiers' gaze as she passed them in the streets. They numbered about six hundred under General Harney. Everyone knew their mission was to wipe out the Indians.

✦ ✦ ✦

WHEN they left the fort, Kate rode backwards in the wagon, holding paper and pencils on her lap and teaching Constance and Ella Spruill how to draw, a bumpy endeavor. Just past a grain mill, a dot appeared and grew until it became a man running toward them. He was covered in flour, and he kept looking over his shoulder. Kate couldn't help but laugh. She read his face and found nothing to fear.

"Come on up," she said. "Is somebody chasing you?"

"My boss, but I think he gave up."

He swung himself on board. His name was Hank Charles. He helped with the animals and paid for a ferry crossing, and as they moved deeper into Indian country, where the natives wanted guns, he pacified them with wire and gunpowder.

One day, several Sioux blocked the trail and pointed to Susan Edmiston.

"They like your hair," Hank said. "They want it."

Susan untied her ribbons and offered them. The Indians held up a knife. James stepped in front of her.

Hank spoke to the Indians and said to James, "Bring out the whiskey, quick."

Peace was maintained, and later, Susan joked if her hair was going to be that troublesome, she should cut it off. She trembled as Olivia braided it. Kate's own hair was light brown, long and shiny, but nobody would ever crave it as a trophy. That was one advantage to being plain.

One morning, Hank spotted a wagon train in the distance. "Think I'll run up ahead."

"You're in a hurry, aren't you?" Kate was sorry to see him go.

"Reckon so." He jumped off, and that was goodbye.

+ + +

THEY traveled through long hours of summer light, stopped at noon, and moved again until day's end. Sharp stubs of dry grass irritated the feet of the oxen and the cow. Mr. Spruill cleansed the wounds and applied ointment, and the party lay by for three days so they could improve. Kate felt overwhelmed with anxiety. She tried to talk to Olivia, but she was silent and withdrawn, exhausted, Kate figured. She was glad when they set out again.

A towering landmark became visible at the horizon. For days, it beckoned, seeming to float above the flat earth. This was Chimney Rock, 250 miles past Fort Kearny. When they finally reached it, they joined other travelers milling around in hushed awe. A single pyramidal hill rose from scoured earth, topped by a three-hundred-foot rock pillar.

"Pointing to heaven," Martin said. Kate was surprised. He rarely spoke of God.

"The Indians call it the elk's cock," James said.

After they left, they kept looking back. The youngest Spruill children cried when they couldn't see it anymore.

+ + +

One evening when Kate and Olivia were fixing supper, a woman approached, her face flaring into the firelight. Gray hair snagged at her shoulders.

"I lost 'em," she said, "them I was with."

"Eat," Kate offered, "and come with us tomorrow. We're bound to catch up with them."

"I'll just stretch out a while."

The woman lay on her back. The toes of her boots made black peaks against the sunset. Kate set a bowl of beans near her, and biscuits with honey. They were using all their supplies now. In the morning, the woman and the food were gone.

"If she can't find them," Kate said, "what'll she do?"

"You can't worry about everybody," Olivia said.

When had the glory seeped out of the days? Beneath the endless sky, Kate felt like a mouse hunted by hawks.

✦ ✦ ✦

THE land soared as they entered the Laramie Range. Dust caked their mouths, eyes, and noses. The horned skulls of cattle and buffalo littered the cracked earth. Farther on, they passed Independence Rock, which looked like a giant stone turtle. At Devil's Gate Canyon, where the Sweetwater River flowed, they drank and filled their casks. Next was the South Pass. A steep descent followed. The oxen slipped on the rocks, and everyone was out and walking.

"Only eight hundred miles to go," Martin said.

On a level stretch, the oxen broke into a run. The horses and mules ran too, and the cow, until they reached a shallow pond.

"Don't let them drink," James yelled.

The men kicked and spurred their mounts so they'd run around the water, but there was no stopping the oxen. They plowed into the pond, dragging the wagons with them. The cow plunged in, and they drank their fill while the men shouted and lashed with whips.

Within an hour, the cow strained at the rope that tethered her to the Spruills' wagon, broke away, and ran. Zachary Willis gave chase but returned without her. James called an early halt, and the men searched in vain for good water.

In the morning, two of the oxen were dead. Thanks to the spare pair, there were still enough to pull the four wagons. In the searing sunlight, Kate looked at a map and felt sick.

"Should we turn back?" she asked Martin. "Can we?"

"No. We've come too far."

When they stopped at midday, two more oxen sank down. The Sibleys would all have to share a wagon. To make room, Olivia and Kate discarded cooking things and furniture, but it would still be crowded. The couples would take turns sleeping in the wagon and underneath it, on a rubber mat.

One moment, Olivia was beside her, frying bread in bacon grease, and the next she was gone, and so was James. Kate blinked. Did no one else notice? Didn't Andrew?

"Should we butcher them?" Martin asked, pointing to the two oxen, now dead.

"We need the meat," said James, who was nearby after all.

Olivia and Susan were talking, their heads bent together. Jealousy struck Kate's heart, sharp as a claw. She, not Susan, had worked with Olivia on the farm. Together they'd wrenched their backs and blistered their hands.

James turned the knobs on his banjo and picked out a tune.

✦　✦　✦

ZACHARY Willis rode ahead all day and slept out in the open. He did his share of the work and more, and as grass became scarcer, they relied on him to scout it out. When the other men's hair grew long, they asked the women to cut it, but he didn't bother. From the back, he might have been an Indian.

Hannah Spruill turned sixteen. A long-legged tomboy when they'd started, she had grown womanly. Laughing, she twined daisies into a chain and slipped it over Zachary's head. Ten years older, he protested but gave her a smile.

They made Fort Bridger and forged northwest into the Idaho territory, pausing at hot springs, where the burning water tasted like metal and did not slake thirst. Nearly everyone contracted a miserable fever, with sore throat and aching muscles. When Kate felt better, she craved sausage and fried apples, but there weren't any. The gristly ox meat had spoiled. They picked worms out of their bacon and rationed the rice, beans, and hardtack.

Kate and Martin no longer sought each other out for lovemaking. She felt too filthy and tired, and Martin fell asleep without reaching for her. What might be going on in the other wagons was a mystery. She felt empty inside, as if she'd been in the Rocky Mountains forever.

The oxen struggled up the steep, stony paths. Mr. Spruill complained of stomachache. As it worsened, his moans reached every ear. When night fell, Kate took a lantern to the Spruills' wagon and offered to sit up with him. Mrs. Spruill burrowed into the wagon and soon was snoring. Hannah and Zachary joined Kate, Hannah's eyes huge with fear, and they kept vigil through the night. Kate listened to Hannah tell Zachary about the food she would cook when they reached Oregon.

"Blueberry muffins," Hannah said. "Would you like that?"

"I sure would," Zachary said.

"I can make chicken pie. Ma taught me. Do you like chicken pie?"

"I sure do."

In the morning, Mr. Spruill was well enough to sit up and drink tea, and they gave him the last of the sugar. In a stretch of well-watered country, Martin shot an antelope, and the fresh meat heartened them. As if drawn by the savory smell, a group of Iowans appeared, and Kate's party offered to share. The guests contributed dried pears and cherry wine, and the food was passed from hand to hand in a welcome respite. They camped together that night. In the morning, the Iowans pushed off early. Some fear nagged at Kate, a sense her group had taken a risk, but the visitors had looked healthy, even robust, without contagion or infirmity.

Soon they would reach Fort Hall, the junction with the California Trail, where the Edmistons would leave them. Kate looked into her heart and asked herself if she could stop loving James. He was a mirage, like clouds that promised rain but were only dust.

When they stopped at noon, Olivia summoned Kate and Mrs. Spruill.

"Susan's baby is coming," Olivia said.

Susan labored for eighteen hours, until, just before daybreak, she delivered a little boy. Mrs. Spruill washed and swaddled him.

"Someday," Olivia said, "we'll tell him he was born on the Oregon Trail."

Kate felt as tired as if she'd had a baby herself.

"I'll go find James and tell him he has a son," she said, but a pain in her stomach drove her to her knees.

It was cholera. For days, she lay delirious, barely aware of others offering water, her fever dreams haunted by the jolly supper with strangers. She must have drunk the water, because she began to revive. Recovery brought bitter revelations. Mr. Spruill, Hannah, and Susan's infant had all died. Martin was sick. Kate held a cup of water to his lips and waited a long moment before he opened his eyes and drank. She kissed his forehead and thanked God it was cool.

Andrew, James, and Zachary buried the dead. They weren't strong enough to dig deep graves, so they hacked into the trail. Wheels would pack the earth and keep animals from digging up the bodies. They left no markers, not even rocks.

✦ ✦ ✦

THERE was no remedy for the time they had lost except to push on. Everyone had lost weight, and their clothes hung off them, but no one looked worse than James and Susan. His eyes were sunken, her face was puffy, and her breasts leaked pitifully through her dress.

Billy Spruill shot three jackrabbits, so there was a good meal for the first time in days. The Edmistons sat apart from the others, with their own fire. Since the baby's death, they had kept to themselves.

Olivia set down her tin plate. "Andrew and I are going with James and Susan," she said.

Kate stared at her. "To California?"

"Yes."

"But we've got to stick together."

"Come with us," Olivia said.

"We'll take the Hudspeth Cutoff," Andrew said. "It's the fastest way."

"What are you talking about?" Martin said. "We've said Oregon all along."

"We changed our minds," Andrew said. "After harvest-time, I'll do a little prospecting."

For a few minutes, they ate in silence. Kate couldn't swallow.

"I don't hear much good about the Hudspeth," Martin said.

"Won't be worse than what we been through," Andrew said.

"You'll have to go over high mountains, and there's not much water."

"We'll take it quick." Andrew dug into his stew. "What about y'all?" he asked Mrs. Spruill and Zachary.

"I ain't changing horses in the middle of the race," Mrs. Spruill said.

"I either," Zachary's first words since Hannah's burial.

Andrew shrugged. *I'm sorry I married him,* Olivia had said before they started. Kate grabbed her hand.

"Let him go," she whispered. "Let them all go. Stay with us."

"I'd worry too much." Olivia looked toward the Edmistons, slumped at their fire.

"You'd pick them over your own flesh and blood?"

"You'll be fine, but they might not be. I want to go."

Kate jumped to her feet and stormed over to the Edmistons. Startled, their heads snapped up, their eyes shiny in the smoky light, and Susan flung out her hands, reading Kate's face.

"We didn't do anything," Susan said. "It's up to them."

"You played on her sympathies," Kate said.

Martin was right behind her. "Now is not the time to be splitting up. Come with us, and go to California later."

"We just want to get there," James said, "and the sooner the better."

Gaunt and diminished, he was only a commonplace sort of man. His shrunken frame, his silence where music and song had been, awakened her pity, and she retreated, sick at heart. Martin took Andrew aside, and they argued. When Martin came back, he was shaking his head.

"They're going," he said. "I told him, at least get with a bigger group."

Three days later, they reached the Hudspeth Cutoff, and the wagons veered apart—Andrew, Olivia, and the Edmistons in one, and Kate, Martin, Zachary, and the Spruills in the others, moving fast on a flat stretch. The two groups waved and hollered. The sounds were jubilant, but Kate couldn't stand it. She leaped out and ran across the rutted earth.

Perched on the back of the wagon, Olivia didn't budge. Kate kept running toward her until she eased down into the road. Kate clung to her, sobbing, while the wagons rolled away. Olivia's neck and shoulder blades felt thin and knobby under Kate's hands. Olivia wept too, but when the others slowed and came back, she went with the Edmistons.

✦ ✦ ✦

IN November 1855, Kate, Martin, Zachary, Mrs. Spruill, and her four surviving children arrived in the Willamette Valley. Martin and Kate staked out a parcel of land, Zachary claimed land of his own, and he and Martin helped each other build houses. In the spring, they plowed and planted. Mrs. Spruill set up a lunchroom in Salem, and Kate and Martin ate there whenever they went into town.

Mail began to arrive, but none from Olivia. Kate wrote to newspapers and courthouses in San Francisco and Sacramento, to the makeshift post offices in the gold fields, to everyone she knew in Virginia, and to newspapers and churches in Kentucky, hoping to locate the Edmistons' kin, but no one had heard anything. She put up a sign in Mrs. Spruill's restaurant seeking word of *Andrew and Olivia Sibley, James and Susan Edmiston, Hudspeth Cutoff, October 1855*. There were many signs like that. Salem buzzed with tales of reunions. People might be lost or delayed for months, and then they'd show up somewhere. Kate tried to stay hopeful, but worry and guilt sickened her. She kept imagining Olivia, Andrew, James, and Susan lying in the snow.

At Christmastime, 1856, she had a baby boy. In the spring, she took him to Mrs. Spruill's restaurant. *Chicken pie, Beef steak, Corn fritters* read the chalkboard outside. She pushed the door open. In the noisy, fragrant lunchroom, Billy and George were waiting tables, and Constance and Ella swept the floors, working the broom around diners' feet.

"They're city kids now," Mrs. Spruill said. She reached for the baby and held him.

"I brought a new sign," Kate said. She took the old tattered one down and tacked the new one on the wall. Mrs. Spruill eyed it.

"Olivia's strong," she said. "If they got over, it's because of her."

"She didn't owe them that. She didn't owe them her life."

Billy dropped a tray, plates smashed, and customers looked up and boisterously cheered. The scene barely registered on Kate.

"Her and Andrew wasn't well-matched," Mrs. Spruill said. "A guiding light and a little puppy dog."

Her face showed perception, and Kate grasped at that. "They had a chance to part ways."

"Some people can take on others' burdens. She knew you'd be all right, and you are."

On their knees, Billy and George were picking up broken plates and cups and stacking the shards on the tray, while Constance and Ella mopped the floor. They were laughing, and the merriment deepened Kate's grief. She might have been sleepwalking all those miles, for all she knew of what was in the others' hearts.

"It didn't mean she didn't love you," Mrs. Spruill said.

Billy hefted the full tray and went back to the kitchen, his brother and sisters joined hands and bowed, and the diners clapped. Mrs. Spruill watched her children steadily.

"They never talk about Hannah or their father," she said.

✦ ✦ ✦

KATE and Martin could hire a search party, but it would cost so much.

"We've got to," he said one night when they'd tossed and turned.

"How would they know where to look?"

"They'd go up in the mountains, past that cutoff, and look for things we might recognize. They don't bring back every busted wheel."

Her misery flared. "My sister. Your brother. How could they?"

"They changed their minds," he said. "Thought California'd be nicer."

"They deserted us. For the Edmistons."

"Don't be so hard-hearted, Kate. They weren't trying to get away from us. They wanted us to go with them."

"If only we had."

"And then we'd probably be dead."

They were quiet for a long time. The suffering the others must have endured, the likelihood they were gone, shamed the anger out of her.

"Didn't you feel some way about him?" he said. "James?"

"No." She swallowed hard. *I didn't love him very long.*

"I always thought you did."

"No." *And whatever Olivia may have felt, or the others, I won't blame them for it.*

✦ ✦ ✦

MARTIN found a tracker who had a good reputation, and he and Kate provided a description of Andrew, Olivia, the Edmistons, and their wagon. The tracker and his crew were gone for months. When they came back, they lugged three big crates into the parlor.

"From different spots in the mountains. Animals scattered the bones."

Kate and Martin tore the crates open. Bridle, kettle, box of fish-hooks. Gunstock, old boot, bent spoon, the ground-down detritus of the trail. Everything smelled of mud and char. Had the trackers just scavenged dumps and ditches around Salem? Dishonest searchers were known to do that. Yet the things did seem to give off the trail's menace. As Martin examined a mashed saddle, dirt flaked off and stained the parlor rug.

"Nothing is theirs." Kate allowed her dread to give way to a measure of relief.

Martin sorted through the last crate and lifted out a banjo.

"That was in a ravine," the lead tracker said. "I clambered down for it."

The strings were broken and curled. When Martin turned it over, a design flashed up on the back of the fingerboard. Kate gasped. He passed it to her, and it felt light and cold. She ran her fingertips over the shiny white flowers. *Mother-of-pearl.*

"It's his, isn't it?" Martin said.

He paid the men, and they left. Dry-mouthed, Kate sat down and cradled the banjo, picking at the strings. She could almost feel James's fingers on hers.

"Well, now we know," Martin said.

"It can't be the only one like it."

Their son ran in and started to play with the relics. Martin shooed him out and tossed them back into the crates. *Clunk, clunk.*

"Maybe they threw things away to lighten the load," she said. "We did that all the time, remember? Maybe they're fine. They got where they were going, and . . ."

"Don't, Kate. Let this be the end of it."

"But . . ." She bent her head over the banjo and cried.

He grabbed it and broke it over his knee.

✦ ✦ ✦

THE long-expected war disrupted the mail and put an end to emigration. She gave birth to a daughter and another son. As the children grew up, she told them about the trail's hardships and beauty, but she was still trying to figure out the other stories, the ones in her heart.

Terror gnawed at her, even though it was years too late. At times, even with her new life unfurling before her, she was back at that fork in the trail, jumping off the wagon to run to Olivia. She would grow old with wondering, aching about the last time she saw her. No matter if she lived to be ninety, she would never get over it. How could she have let her go? There must have been something she could have done or said.

The trail ate a hole in her heart. She quit talking about it. She hated the trail and her younger self for not knowing how to hold on to the sister she loved so much.

The wagons had moved apart with surprising speed, churning up dust. The roads diverged and the gap stretched wide. Her feet pounded the earth. Olivia rode on the back of the Edmistons' wagon with her legs dangling. Kate kept running, trying to close the distance.

Shades

WARREN SAW THE GIRL before she saw him. He was waiting in the parking lot of the barbecue place for his daddy and Aunt Tate, had been waiting a long time when the girl came out, balancing Styrofoam containers against her chest. He liked her red-and-gold T-shirt. She went to a white car and put the food on the passenger seat.

She closed the door, and then she saw him. She had a serious look about her, the way Warren felt much of the time, even when he played with his toys or his kittens. His daddy laughed a lot, to cover up his sadness, but he was serious when he sat down on the back porch, tired after mowing grass.

The girl came over.

"What are you doing?" she asked.

He poked at the grass with a stick.

"Nothing." He tossed the stick away. "Waiting for Daddy and Aunt Tate."

"You have different eyes."

"I know. One's blue and one's brown."

"Did you eat barbecue?"

"Yes, and I had some French fries. Why did you buy so much?" he said.

"It's for my friends. They gave me money, and I picked it up."

"You must have lots of friends."

A strand of long black hair blew across the girl's lips. She pushed it away. She reminded him of an Indian maiden in a book, but she wore sneakers, not moccasins. The girl in the book had birds flying around her.

"What's your name?" she asked.

"Warren. It's Daddy's name, too."

"I'm Natalie. Is your dad in the restaurant?"

"Yes," he said, angry as he added, "I'm sick of waiting. Aunt Tate spilled stuff on her dress."

"That sauce is messy." Natalie's beautiful face looked serious again. "How old are you?"

"Five."

"Where's your mother?"

"I don't know. At her house, I guess."

"She doesn't live with you?"

"She used to." It hurt to talk about his mama. When he saw her these days, it was only for a little while. She would take him places, maybe to the mall to look at puppies.

"Would you like to take a ride with me while you're waiting?" Natalie said.

"Daddy'd get mad."

"No, he won't. You'll be with me, and we'll have fun."

He looked toward the restaurant, but there was no sign of his daddy or Aunt Tate.

"Can I go tell them?"

"We'll be back so soon." Natalie held out her hand. "By then, your aunt's dress will be clean."

"Okay." He followed her to the car.

She moved the food so he could sit up front. Out on the road, she went fast, passing a pickup truck. Red sauce had leaked from the containers onto the cloth seat.

"That looks like blood," he said, and laughed.

"It's okay. It's not my car. Where do you live?"

"At 4920 Grace Road," he said, the address coming back to him like a song. "The mailbox is a duck. If you have a letter for the mailman, you put its wing up."

They passed a field he loved because it was full of horses. They went through a deep patch of forest where trees arched over the road like a tunnel, and they headed into town.

"Would you like to meet my friends?" she said.

"Okay."

They reached an area Warren recognized. He saw a restaurant with a neon sign he liked, which was lit up even in the daytime—a giant red bug.

"That's a lobster," Natalie said.

"What's a lobster?"

"It's summertime," she said, "summer in Maine when you're feeling free and rich."

The street narrowed as they reached the old part of town. Aunt Tate always said about the red brick buildings: *There's the college.* Natalie parked behind a house. Crumbling pink crape myrtle blossoms drifted down on the windshield.

"We're home," she said. "Toot the horn." He reached over and honked. Natalie laughed and said, "Can you help me unload?"

He was careful with the containers she handed him. As they went around the house, he saw young women all over the porch.

"You took long enough, Natalie," said one girl, with gladness in her voice. "Who's your friend?"

"This is Warren," said Natalie. "Here's your keys."

The glad-voiced woman took the keys. She had thick yellow curls and a red-and-gold cap. She saw Warren notice it.

"I'm Roma. Want to wear this?" She placed the cap on his head.

It covered his eyes. The girls laughed.

"A little big," Roma said, and put it back on.

"I have to go to the bathroom," Warren said.

"I'll show you where it is," Natalie said.

He followed her into the house. It smelled perfumey, and a big TV was on. The bathroom was nice, with gold faucets, and the towels had owls on them. Then he found Natalie in the kitchen, where the girls were unpacking the food and pouring Coke into paper cups.

"Have some, Warren," Roma said. To Natalie, she said, "Okay, who is he?"

"My nephew."

"What's a nephew?" he said.

The girls chuckled.

"You're an only child, Natalie," Roma said. "How can you have a nephew?"

"I'm friends with his parents," Natalie said. "They asked me to watch him for a while."

"He's a cutie," said a girl whose cheeks made apple shapes when she smiled. "My name's Jennifer," she told him.

Warren drank his Coke. He liked all the girls.

"It's a big day for us, Warren," Roma said. "We're in Rush Week. Has Natalie told you what that is?"

"No." He gazed around the kitchen. The fridge was white and extra-big. Everything was clean, except where barbecue sauce had spilled. Some of the girls smoked cigarettes, leaning their heads back and laughing as they blew smoke into the air.

"Rush Week," said Roma, "is when we choose who else will be in our club. It's fun, but it's heartbreaking too, because there are so many girls, and we can't take all of them."

"Why not?" he said, yet knowing you couldn't get everything you wanted.

"Silly rules are why." Roma raised the Coke bottle toward him.

"He's had enough," said Natalie. "I promised not to let him have too much sugar."

"Ohh," said Roma, breaking into a yawn. She pushed her plate away, pillowed her head on her arms, and said in a muffled voice, "If y'all want to rest up before the parties, do it now. We've got to be tip-top."

"Warren, do you want to see my room?" Natalie asked.

"Yes," he said, as Daddy and Aunt Tate popped into his mind. He wondered if they were still inside the restaurant. He followed Natalie up the steps. On the walls above the stairs were group photos of the girls at railroad tracks.

"A choo-choo train!" he said.

"That's one of our symbols," Natalie said. "It's in a song I'll teach you."

Her room was wonderful. Sunlight turned the curtains golden, like the bands on her shirt, and she had bunk beds. He reached for the top one.

"Let me give you a boost." She lifted him. "You're heavier than you look."

From the top bunk, he surveyed her dresser, crowded with sparkly jewelry. In a corner stood an easel with bright colors splashed on canvas. Suitcases were stacked against a wall.

"Are you going on a trip, Natalie?"

"I made trips all summer," she said. "I went to California with a guy, a ski coach. We got married and drove all over the country. Then we split up."

"Oh. Where is he?"

"He's not here. He was never here. Nobody sleeps in that bunk. My roommate decided not to come back this year."

Something shiny hung on the bedpost—a crown, set with bright clear stones.

"Are you a queen, Natalie?"

"I was the Queen Bee at the Honey Festival back home." She pulled open her closet door. "Here's my gown."

She held up a long shimmering dress made of layers and layers of floaty cloth.

"It looks like clouds," he said, "or butterfly wings." He reached out to touch the soft, dazzling material, which had tiny golden bees stitched to silver netting. He loved the dress and the way she was smiling. "What did you do when you were the queen?"

"I gave away little jars of honey at fairs." She hung the dress in the closet. "Let's draw."

"Are you a good draw-er?"

"The best. I'm an art major."

From her desk, she took crayons, colored pencils, and paper, and spread them on the floor. He climbed off the bunk and settled beside her.

"Don't tell the others what I told you," she said. "About being married. They don't know."

He didn't see why that had to be a secret. "Okay."

She sketched a man with long poles on his feet, flying off a mountainside.

"Have you ever gone skiing?" she asked.

"No," he said, thinking Aunt Tate's dress would be clean by now. They'd be out in the parking lot, maybe home. "I have to go back."

"Please, not yet." She looked sad. "Aren't you having fun? We'll play—we'll play some more."

She lifted the sparkly necklaces and earrings from her dresser and piled them on his lap. She took jars of glitter, sequins, and confetti, and tossed handfuls into the air so they rained down brilliantly. He laughed, catching glitter in his hands, on his tongue. It tasted like the tinsel on a Christmas tree. She set the heavy, jeweled crown on his head, but it fell off. He spat glitter into his hand.

Somebody knocked on the door. Apple-cheeked Jennifer stuck her head in and said, "Natalie, we need you downstairs. You're supposed to be a greeter."

"Can't somebody take my place?" Natalie said.

"Hurry up," said Jennifer.

"Get Kimberly or Heidi to do it," said Natalie, but Warren sensed she wasn't talking to Jennifer, who had already gone away, or to him. "So many sisters," she said tiredly.

"Are they all your sisters?"

"So they say. Do you have brothers and sisters?"

"No. I wish I had 'em."

"You have me," she said. "I'm going downstairs now. I'll be back soon."

Warren found he was sleepy. He scrambled up to the top bunk by himself this time, and she climbed high enough to kiss his cheek.

"I love you," she said. "I don't know why I'm going down at all."

✦ ✦ ✦

ROMA adored Rush Week: these fevered days. She was talking with an eager girl whose braces shone like crushed dimes and whose mascaraed lashes brushed her brows when she blinked. For some time, Roma had been standing in the official distress position—hand on hip—but none of her sisters had come to her aid. She excused herself just as the bell rang, indicating the end of the party. In five minutes, another group of rushees would burst in. She reveled in these parties, even when she got stuck with somebody dull.

She felt drunk and didn't know why. She did not, as some of the girls did, spike her punch cup. Alcohol was against the rules. So was having anybody in the house besides sisters and rushees.

In the bathroom, she splashed water on her face—her homely face, but she was used to it—and adjusted her nametag, a cardboard owl with folded wings. The little boy wasn't supposed to be here, but nobody would criticize Natalie. Nobody ever did. She was too beautiful and scandalous; she was beyond this world. She hadn't cared whether or not she got in, so every sorority on campus had been mad for her, and Roma, setting her cap for the presidency, had led a great conquest. Once Natalie was in, she made fun of the rituals and stole everybody's boyfriend, even Roma's, a shy physics major. Natalie cast her spell, trifled with him, and dumped him. He had never come back to Roma.

At least Natalie had asked to borrow Roma's car today before picking up the barbecue. She didn't want to risk spilling sauce in her own car. She'd said so, and Roma had handed her the keys, as she always did. The seats were splattered and stained from all the times Natalie hadn't even asked.

Well, what to do? Roma could find out the child's address and take him home herself. It was strange: she'd felt a sense of recognition when she saw him coming around the yard, as if he belonged to her. In fact, she had felt a piercing, painful love, so when she laid her head on the kitchen table and talked about resting up for the party, she'd really wanted to cry.

She should have expected Natalie to do exactly this. Often when a group of girls were out and about—at the candy store where tourists jostled for sweets, or at the deli where sandwiches were named for the college dormitories—there'd be a particularly cute child feasting on a sundae, or a toddler flailing underfoot while its distracted parents dithered about burgers. Natalie would stop in her tracks and say, *Oh, I'd like to steal that little thing.* The other girls laughed, but Roma discerned a hint of craziness in the lilting voice and mournful gaze. She'd imagined Natalie snatching an infant from its mother's arms or seizing a youngster from a schoolyard.

Natalie must have found Warren at the barbecue joint. She was a criminal, she ought to be in jail, his parents must be frantic. Roma had to figure out how to get Warren back to safety and keep the sorority out of trouble, but the next wave of girls was surging through the door, violently cheery.

She dried her face on an owl-themed towel and stepped into the hall. She liked all the girls, even those who sent her hand to her hip. She didn't want college ever to end, because then the rush parties would be over, and every autumn of her life, she would miss them.

She would grow old with missing them.

"Hi, I'm Stephanie," cried a girl in a plaid wool suit. Whoever heard of wearing wool in this climate, the first week of September?

"Where are you from?" Roma asked.

"Alexandria," came the answer. Or had she said Winchester? Roma's ears buzzed with the soprano clamor. "I'm a business major, unless I switch to poli sci."

"We do stress scholarship in our sorority," Roma said.

"If I don't get in, I'm going to kill myself." The girl flexed her red-frosted lips.

"Some have," said Roma, as sweat crept from the edges of the plaid wool.

✦ ✦ ✦

WARREN dreamed about Aunt Tate and the game they played on hot evenings. They were out in the backyard and Aunt Tate was making an arc of water with the garden hose. *Under the rainbow,* she called it. He raced back and forth under the waterfall until Aunt Tate turned the hose on him full blast, driving him down to the grass. It felt ticklish, cool, and wonderful.

There in the quiet, sunlit room, he woke up and remembered about Natalie. Merry voices drifted through the floorboards. He wanted to find Natalie and learn the choo-choo song. He climbed down from the bunk and went downstairs into a crowd of flowered sundresses.

A girl knelt beside him and said, "Whose boy are you?" She had freckles on her nose and clinky bracelets on her arm.

"I'm Warren."

The girls laughed, looking around at the others with raised eyebrows.

Roma appeared, her blonde curls gone frizzy, and put a hand on his shoulder.

"Let's get you some punch," she said, but the gladness had gone out of her voice.

The punch was pink, with slices of lemon floating in it. There were cookies and gumdrops in crystal bowls, which Roma offered to him. Natalie came over, shaking glitter out of her black hair, and swooped down to hug him.

"Did you have a good nap?" she said.

"Natalie, you should have changed out of your jeans," Roma said. "You know the rules."

"Oh, fiddle," Natalie said. "I didn't want to come back to these stupid parties. Guess what? I got married."

Roma's cheeks turned pink like the punch.

"You really did? Who?"

Natalie paused. "Oh, it's just a joke."

"Funny," Roma said, but she wasn't laughing.

"Warren, Roma is very important," Natalie said. "She's our president."

"Oh," he said, but somehow he felt she was making fun of Roma. "Natalie's a queen. Did you know that?" he said to Roma.

Natalie knelt down and clasped his hands, her grip warm and tight.

"I'll take good care of you," she said.

He gazed back at her, his mouth tasting of peppermint gumdrops. His stomach rumbled.

"I heard that little tummy growl," she said. "We'll have pizza after the last party. What do you like on yours?"

"Green peppers."

"Me too," Natalie said. He was surprised to see tears in her eyes.

"Where do you live, Warren?" Roma asked.

"At 4920 Grace Road," he said.

Roma nodded slowly. "I think I know where that is. Is it near a grocery store?"

"Yes."

Natalie pulled him against her hip and held him there. Her legs felt as slim and sturdy as the young trees in his backyard. She and Roma were arguing. He tried to follow what they were saying, but all he understood was they were mad because of him.

"Haven't you ever seen somebody and just loved them?" Natalie said. "I saw his eyes and I had to. I knew he could love me back."

"You are so selfish," Roma said. "How do you think his parents feel right now? If you take him home right now, I won't tell anybody."

"Don't fight," said Warren. He was thinking of the way his mama and daddy used to get so mad at each other.

"It's all right, Warren," said Natalie. "We're at a party. We're having fun."

"I had a dream," he said, the happiness of that dream coming back to him. "Aunt Tate was making a rainbow in the yard."

But somebody tapped Natalie on the shoulder and she turned away, so it was Roma who bent down to listen to him.

✦   ✦   ✦

IN the breaks between parties, when there were only sisters in the house, the kitchen was the place to be. Girls shrieked as they plunged their bare feet into a tub of ice water, churning it up and down, yelling as they slipped ice cubes down each other's backs. Climbing out of the tub, they groaned as they rubbed ice across their cheeks and foreheads and arms.

A current of fire ran from Roma's heels all the way to her scalp—exhaustion or adrenaline, she didn't know which. There had been seven parties in five hours. One more, only one, to go. She ordered two sophomores to drag the tub out and dump it in the yard. The others scurried to find their shoes in the heap on the kitchen floor.

She closed her eyes as the bell rang again, the next-to-last rush bell she would ever hear. The bell at the end of this party would be the last.

It was her senior year, and life as she knew it was ending, swift as the ice water was melting into the soft earth out in the yard. After the last party, there would be the grand finale, Porch Routine, when all the sorority girls tried to out-sing and out-dance the other sororities, and the audience, hundreds of bedazzled rushes, rocked back and forth in the courtyard, yearning, trying to sing along with the house they wanted to join, there in the searing sun of a September evening. Roma had drilled her girls all week, limbering them up, so they could line up on the old stone porch and cheer their lungs out, always smiling, luring the ones who would be campus stars, who would keep it all going next year and the year after that and forever.

The ice water had worked. Roma could no longer feel the blisters on her feet.

All around her, girls whooped, smoothed back their hair, and raced to their places in the living room and the front hallway to greet the final group of rushees. Yet Roma couldn't move. She heard fifty first-year women thronging into the house, their earrings rattling as loud as their greetings. The smell of hair spray and nail polish was a drug in her nose, the owl nametag on her chest beat its wings as fast as her heart, her period announced itself between her legs, the roof of the house lifted off—and there she was in the kitchen with Warren, who said, "Natalie went to wash her hair. Do you like green peppers, Roma?"

✦   ✦   ✦

WHEN it was all over, after Porch Routine had gone into encores and their throats were raw, the sisters swept back into their houses and left the courtyard full of applauding rushees. All the porches emptied at the same time; it was the rules. The rushees streamed away in hope and despair to await what the next day might bring: coveted white cards in formal script, inviting them to smaller, more select parties, whereas the initial round, strictly timed, was open to all.

For many, there would be cards from the wrong house, or no cards at all.

Inside, Roma listened for the next stage—exhausted silence. Sighing, the girls headed upstairs, where they peeled off their party clothes and put on denim shorts with their red-and-gold T-shirts. Roma had already called the pizza man, and he had delivered a sizeable order. The girls crept down to the kitchen, opened the warm cardboard boxes, heaped their plates, and retired to eat on the porch swing or the balcony. Cicadas chanted in the courtyard trees.

Some of the girls ate in their rooms, where the twilight breeze lifted the curtains up and down in time with their breathing and floor fans blew across the shag rugs so photos of boyfriends, stuck in mirror frames, took wing. Wearily the girls traded mushrooms and pepperoni like charms. There was beer, too, in icy bottles that they rolled gratefully across their necks.

Roma had allowed Warren to watch Porch Routine from Natalie's window, and then she had shepherded him out to her car, intending to take him home, or maybe to the police station, she hadn't decided. But Natalie ran out begging, *Let me, please let me.* And Roma had given in.

Back in the kitchen, she trembled all over.

A few of the girls—Jennifer, Heidi, and Kimberly—carried their food into the living room and turned the TV on. Warren's face bloomed on the screen. With a collective gasp, the girls looked at each other, jumped up, and crowded around a phone.

Roma dove into their huddle and snatched it away.

"It's just a little mix-up," she said. "Natalie has taken him home. They just left."

"But he's been reported as a missing child," insisted Kimberly, a last-year's pledge with a stubborn mouth.

"You let her drive away with him?" Heidi screeched.

"Go finish your supper." Roma put steel in her voice.

"I bet you gave her your car," Kimberly said. "That makes you an accessory."

"It's fine. It's all over."

Of course it wasn't over. Roma's knees were weak. She should have let them call the police, should have made the call herself. Even if Natalie did take him home, his parents would get the story out of him. Innocently he would tell about the parties and the singing. He would name names, and the authorities would come. In a few hours, maybe even a few minutes, Roma would be in as much trouble as Natalie was—and that was the best Roma could hope for.

Yet Kimberly and Heidi retreated. Roma remembered how, at the initiation ceremony, Kimberly had tripped and staggered in her long white gown, and Roma had despised her a little.

Jennifer stood her ground. "Natalie kidnapped a child."

"She was babysitting."

"That's a lie. And you don't know where she might have taken him."

"I never want to hear another word about it," Roma said.

"You're covering up for her."

Under Jennifer's blazing eyes, Roma quaked.

Warren had hugged Roma as they walked out to her car. By then, she had wanted to hide him, to pitch everything away and run off with him, with Natalie too if that was what it took. The pizza man had arrived, pulling up beneath the crape myrtles. A little gentleman, Warren put out his hand, and the pizza man shifted the boxes in his arms and shook it, and Roma and Natalie looked at each other above Warren's head and burst out laughing. Warren was so young and the man was so old. *I've delivered pizza to this house for forty years,* he said. They stood there with crape myrtle blossoms floating down on their heads, and Natalie said, *Let me, let me,* and slipped the keys out of Roma's limp fingers.

Jennifer's gaze skewed to the door. "The cops are here!"

Shapes of people on the porch showed through the sheer curtains. The bell rang, and three women stepped inside, matrons in pastel linen with corsages on their lapels.

"Oh, my Lord," Jennifer breathed. "It's . . . it's . . ."

"The national officers," Roma said.

She moved forward and made introductions. The words came automatically. Thanks to the sorority handbook, she had memorized the names and faces, down to the mole on the chin of Mrs. Jean Jelpy, President. The others were Mrs. Louise Whitecliff, Vice President, and Mrs. Georgina Powers, Secretary.

"We are so honored," Roma said.

This would be a legend. For years, girls would talk about *the time the national officers just showed up.*

"We can't stay," the women said. "Bring us wonderful pledges this year, like you always do, girls like yourselves. We're counting on you.

We keep track of you from our headquarters, far away from this lovely place. You are our favorite chapter in the country, the whole world."

"Let's sing one song," said Mrs. Georgina Powers. She settled on the piano bench and launched into the anthem. She pressed the pedals so the chords sounded deep and slow. Pewter hair bobbed free from her chignon.

Roma closed her eyes and sang. Others joined in. Like divas, the officers loosed their full-throated vigor.

The anthem was never sung in Porch Routine. It was too sad, and it was secret, a song about reunions when they were all unimaginably old, when evening was coming down around them like shades. Roma smelled the officers' White Shoulders cologne. She would be one of them some day, with varicose veins on her legs and a mink coat in her closet.

You are my favorite in the whole world.

The door opened, and Natalie came in, her head down. She raised her streaked face and found Roma's eyes.

Grace Road, Roma thought, as if she'd been there when Warren crossed the yard and ran to tell his people, *I met a queen.*

Comanche Queen

I

December 1860
Mule Creek, Texas

When Captain Sullivan Ross told his Texas Rangers that the first one to shoot a Comanche Indian would get a brand-new Colt revolver, nineteen-year-old Tommy Kelliher decided the gun ought to be his. In pursuit of Chief Peta Nocona, Tommy and his fellow Rangers found a band of Comanches drying meat at a tributary of the Pease River. They were mostly women, kids, and old folks, but the Rangers attacked anyway. In the midst of the raid, Tommy spotted a blue-eyed woman and called out, "Hey, you."

To another Ranger who leveled his rifle at her, he barked, "Don't shoot."

The woman held a baby. She bared her breasts.

"Americano!" she cried.

As Tommy gripped her rough arm and led her to a cottonwood tree, he wondered if he should lie with her or even wed her. Amid buzzing bullets and shrieking Indians, he entertained and rejected the idea of a future with her a dozen times, and him not even the romantic type. It was crazy, the thoughts you had in war, he would say later. Yet as time passed, he would be flabbergasted by the words that sprang to his lips (*when I first beheld her*) on those occasions that he told of discovering the person who turned out to be Cynthia Ann Parker, a famous missing child. Kidnapped by Comanches, she'd grown up to be the chief's wife, *one of his wives,* Tommy would amend.

"We got him," a soldier yelled.

The Rangers tossed a man high and fired at him. It was the chief. He was alive when he went up, and a dead body when he fell. The Rangers tore off the scalp. Tommy saw it, and so did the woman, who bellowed and gouged her cheeks with her fingernails.

Within minutes, the battle was over.

The Rangers took the woman back to their camp. Captain Ross gave her a stick and asked her to draw Parker's Fort on the ground. Her sketch in the dirt showed her family's compound as it was in 1836. Some shadow of the nine-year-old Cynthia Ann remained within, though she had lived with the Comanches for twenty-four years. That very night, Captain Ross got the word out by telegraph to Governor Sam Houston and every newspaper he could think of.

In a few days, Cynthia's uncle, Colonel Isaac Parker, a rancher from Birdville, showed up to claim her. She stood in sunlight, wearing a calico dress loaned by a camp laundress and hiding her face in her baby's neck.

"Is it her?" Tommy asked Isaac Parker.

She raised her head and regarded the men with burning eyes.

"It's her, all right," said Isaac Parker. "She looks like her daddy, my brother that the Indians killed. Remember me, Cindy Ann?"

"Why is she mad at *us?*" Tommy asked.

Isaac Parker spat a stream of tobacco juice that made the laundress's helper, a mulatto girl named Ruth, leap out of the way.

"She wants to go back to 'em," Isaac said.

"But they's savages," Ruth said.

"How she feels, ain't the way *I'd* feel," Isaac agreed.

"What happened when y'all were attacked?" Tommy asked.

Isaac's face went dark. "Indians showed up at my daddy's stockade, hundreds of them, saying they wanted beef. My brother Benjamin had left the gate open. He went back to the Indians with meat, to give the rest of us time to run." He paused. "And they killed him."

Tommy held out a flask. Isaac drank and said, "Then they killed my daddy, my brother Silas, and the two Frost boys. Tortured them first."

Tommy shook his head.

"They raped our women," Isaac said, "and drug off Cindy Ann, her brother John, and her cousin Rachel, my niece. Rachel got away and wrote a book about it. Recollected everything, even the skunks and turtles she had to eat. We ransomed John after six years, but he ran back to 'em." To Cynthia, he said, "Whatever happened to John?"

She didn't answer.

Tommy's anger surged. "Your uncle asked you a question."

Ignoring them, Cynthia nuzzled her baby.

"Her little brother, Silas Junior, they didn't get him," Isaac said. "Remember Silas, Cynthy Ann? He's got a boy of his own now."

She kept her head down.

"And you've got a little sister who was born after you was took," Isaac said. "Orlena, her name is. What do you think about that?"

She pressed her face against the baby's.

Isaac sighed. "Benjamin ought not to left that gate open."

He held the flask toward Tommy, who said, "I'd be honored if you kept it."

✦   ✦   ✦

THE laundress who had loaned the dress was named Lorna Devereaux ("Poppa was French Canuck"). She and Ruth, her helper, had scrubbed Cynthia's face and washed her matted hair. Cynthia did not submit readily; Ruth zealously held her down. The baby was clean, and Lorna and Ruth had exclaimed about that.

After the meeting with Isaac Parker, Cynthia stumped into the room she shared with Lorna, curled into the corner, and nursed the baby. Lorna was there, resting on a cot.

"Mighty nice of your uncle to come all this way," Lorna said, though she knew Cynthia wouldn't answer.

It was twilight. The men were talking outside. From her cot, Lorna listened.

"Does she really want to go back to the Comanches?" Tommy Kelliher said, and Isaac Parker said, "Son, no good deed . . ."

" . . . goes unpunished," Lorna whispered. Her ears pricked up at the sound of whoops and shouts. Indians, she thought, her mouth going dry.

"She's asleep," Isaac Parker called out. "Come back in the morning," and Lorna understood that news of Cynthia had spread, and people wanted to see her.

"You been took twice, Cindy," Lorna said, her voice hollow in the darkness. "First by Indians, now by whites, and you ain't either one."

There was not a word from the seething, lactating presence in the corner.

Lorna tried again. "Your uncle looked for you for years. Offered a reward, trying to get you back. Nobody'd pay to get *me* back."

Specifically, Lorna meant Tommy Kelliher. She had been in love with him for three days, ever since he'd returned with the woman in tow and a swagger in his step. Lorna was ten years older and had whored around with so many soldiers that she held scant hope of being a prize for anyone. She didn't envy Cynthia her fame, but did begrudge her the love behind the ransom that had never been paid.

The next morning, while Lorna scrubbed clothes and bossed the girl tending the fires beneath boiling pots, Isaac Parker led Cynthia out of the fort, he astride a big horse and her and her baby on the meanest mule in the army. Spectators, who had indeed come back at sunup, cheered and applauded. Isaac Parker tipped his hat, but Cynthia gave no sign. Lorna watched them fade into dots far out on the plains. She let the washing fall from her hands. Tears filmed her eyes and spilled over. Her heart was a rockslide, a wagon train, a circle of fire.

"What's the matter, Lorna?" Tommy said.

"He came all that way for her. Nobody would do that for me."

"Aw, honey."

"I could die, and nobody notice."

"I would," Tommy said.

"You would?" Joy rose up in Lorna's heart. She beamed at him, and together they went to her room.

Ruth took over, stirring the wash and thinking. A captive rescued after twenty-four years—seven years longer than Ruth had been alive—a woman so dirty she'd changed color, and sore headed about being found, and her uncle come to fetch her? Amazing. It was like— the girl struggled to compare. Like something in the Bible. There was another emotion in her heart, too, a welter she couldn't parse.

"She ugly," she said to the suds, "but the baby . . ."

Was darling, she admitted. The child's name was Topsannah. A half-Indian cook had translated: it meant Prairie Flower. Ruth thought of sunflowers and rambling roses. She abandoned the washing, sought out the cook, and asked him what else he knew about Cynthia Ann Parker. He prided himself on being an authority on the white squaw.

"She got two boys by the chief," the cook said. "Quanah, about seventeen years, he's killed men already. Big warrior. Younger son is Pecos. The chief had another wife, a full-blood Comanche woman. They shared him."

Ruth shivered. This was better than what the clapping people got. Let the clothes boil over in the pots. If Lorna didn't care, she didn't have to, either. From an oven, the cook took a pan of bread and offered her a slice.

She bit into it. "How come she do that to her face?"

"Broken heart," the cook said.

Ruth knew what Indians were like. They aimed arrows at people's belly-holes, so if the shot didn't kill, the gut-rot would. And everybody'd heard about Martha Sherman out on Stagg Prairie, nine months pregnant, stabbed and raped by many men. The cook was half-Indian, but nothing like that, she told herself.

"Who got that Colt revolver?" he asked. "The one Sul Ross said he'd give?"

She shook her head. She didn't know or care. The cook touched her cheek, and she lifted yeasty lips to his mouth.

✦ ✦ ✦

IN every town in Tarrant County, children were let out of school to see the Comanche Queen. Muttering, Cynthia clutched her baby and hunched atop a crate. Tears ran down her face. Isaac Parker took the money people handed to him. He didn't ask for it, but he was glad to get it. Journeying wasn't cheap, and he was mad at Cynthia. In all those years, why hadn't she come back on her own?

Just outside of Fort Worth, she bolted from the crate. Skilled at greased-pig chases, men and boys hunted her down and found her behind a livery stable, hacking off her hair with an errand boy's cheese knife.

"Grabbed it right out of my hand," said the boy, his teeth thick with cheddar.

A newspaper reporter took her picture, and it ran in papers throughout Texas. She looked straight at the camera, her expression desolate, Topsannah's mouth latched onto a full bare breast.

At the Birdville ranch, Isaac Parker's wife gave Cynthia the spare room, a Bible, and a cradle Cynthia never used, preferring to keep Topsannah in her arms.

"She won't use the privy," Isaac's wife reported. "Goes out in the woods."

Cynthia ran away. Isaac brought her back. He and his wife threatened and cajoled. She wanted them to call her Nautdah, her damn Indian name. Wanted ashcake and buffalo hump. Kept getting hold of sharp objects. Wept and raved and knifed her breasts.

"We're too old for this," Isaac's wife said. "Turn her loose."

"I can't do that."

Isaac had one last hope. She might do better with her brother Silas, who had a son, Wesley, by a wife who had died. Now he had a beautiful new bride named Katherine. Yes, they could take care of Cynthia, and maybe she'd be happier with a young family.

Isaac put her and the baby on the mule again. This time, he tied her hands to the pommel and wrapped Topsannah in a sling around her chest. During a three days' eastward trek in bleaching springtime sun, he gave himself a headache trying to figure out exactly how the baby was kin to ten-year-old Wesley. Oh hell, they was all Parkers.

"Me Nautdah," came the grim voice behind him.

He thought of Balaam's ass. May as well be the mule talking. He had yearned to reclaim that little bright-haired child, and look how it all turned out. The saddest thing was that nobody was sorrier than her, a thirty-three-year-old squaw. She kept looking back while the high country fell away. A sense of hurry came upon Isaac. He urged his horse to a gallop, knowing hers would follow. Thus, in April 1862, Cynthia Ann Parker reached Van Zandt County at a breakneck run.

II

The Methodist preacher, Reverend Campbell, blessed Silas Parker, who was off to fight the Yankees, and chastised the glowering Cynthia for her failure to be thankful. Ten-year-old Wesley Parker, recovering from measles, thought his aunt's giant hands looked like paws. And did she ever quit nursing that baby?

"Isaac was wore out from her, Reverend," said Wesley's stepmother, Katherine.

Wesley's father, Silas, had a stutter that worsened when he was excited.

"Uncle Isaac looked buh-buh-beat to shit," he agreed.

"I can't understand why this woman is not overjoyed," Reverend Campbell said.

"She duh-don't know the difference between took for wrong and took for right," said Silas.

"Cynthia." The preacher banged on the table, and everybody jumped. "The Comanches killed your pa and grandpa. You saw it," he thundered. "They cut off your grandpa's balls and stuffed them in his mouth."

Cynthia's pupils snapped with fury. Wesley marveled she was kin to him.

Silas packed up his extra clothes. "Kath, honey," he said to his wife, "I'll write to you, and Wesley'll keep watch on Cindy. She'll help you, Kath. She'll suh-settle down."

"No, she won't," said Katherine.

+ + +

AND she didn't. Silas Parker did go to war, leaving Wesley with the womenfolk and Homer, a Negro man they owned. Still weak—he had almost died from measles—Wesley churned butter, hoping the work would bring his strength back. Before he got sick, he used to love riding, running, and singing. He was determined to do those things again.

Katherine tried to teach Cynthia how to spin.

"Pick up that thread and do like I showed you," Katherine said.

"Nautdah," the woman insisted, thumping her chest.

"You're Cynthia Ann Parker," Katherine said, "and Parker women know how to spin. So spin."

Cynthia swatted the wheel. Topsannah stretched her arms toward it.

Wesley had heard rumors that made his stomach shake—the Battle of Pease River was a massacre; most of the warriors were gone on a hunt, and the Rangers slaughtered women and children. Maybe that wasn't a sin if they were Indians.

Wesley feared a full moon, the raiders' moon, people called it. *We're safe here,* his father always said, *the Comanches are way out West,* but he knew stories of whole families murdered, the Youngbloods and the Rippys. Worst of all, Martha Sherman, scalped so thoroughly, not one hair was left on her peeled, bleeding head. She had lived four days, long enough to tell her story and birth a dead baby.

"You're not getting *my* scalp, Cynthy Ann," Katherine said.

Wesley laughed. Once he started, he couldn't stop, even when Katherine slapped him. Leaping away, he upset the churn, and butter slid out onto the floor. He was glad for the slap. She wouldn't have done that when he was about to die.

✦ ✦ ✦

CYNTHIA did learn to spin. One moment, she'd be at the wheel, her thick fingers busy with wool, but if Wesley so much as blinked, she was a streak of calico in the yard while the wheel yet hummed. He yelled for Homer, who clattered out of the barn with the mule hitched to the wagon. Wesley clambered over the side. Chickens scattered, and sheepdogs mobbed the wheels. Wesley hung on as the wagon bumped over gopher holes, chasing the distant, bobbing scrap that was Nautdah.

"I'd like to race her," Wesley shouted.

Homer laughed. "She faster than you ever be."

It became a routine. She hid beef jerky and dried apple slices in her sleeves and made an all-out sprint for the Pease River. Each time, she got a little closer to the Plains. Wesley began to hope she'd outrun them. From a distance, she looked like a jackrabbit. Homer said there were prairie ghosts, shape-shifters. They caught her every time. She hoisted herself and the baby onto the wagon. Homer drove slow on the way back and sometimes sang. Wesley did too, "Listen to the Mocking-bird," though he didn't have breath to last to the end.

Did she hate him? He was a spy, a guard, a tattletale. Katherine hated her so much, it made Wesley feel bad, and she called the baby the Little Barbarian.

One day, a cowboy showed up with a cut on his arm and blood on his shirt. He'd been attacked by a tramp, he said. Katherine gave him bandages. "I heard about that white squaw," he said. "Lemme see her."

Wesley led his aunt onto the porch. The cowboy spoke strange words that must have been Indian, and she threw herself at the man's feet, talking back and forth with him.

"She wants me to take her back to the Comanches," he said. "Says she's too old to turn white."

"If she took a bath now and then, she could," Katherine said.

The man laughed. Nautdah retreated to a corner and nursed Topsannah. Wesley saw the man get an eyeful, but she was an animal with its young: the man turned away, bored. Katherine asked him where his home was. She put her hands into her hair, shaking it back. Wesley's father called her Frisky sometimes: *Fr-fr-frisky.*

His father, out in the world.

Wesley wanted to go out in the world. Did that change when a person got older? Hunger to go home—that's what Nautdah felt, though what was her home but a trail of wild game?

"I'm from west Texas," the man said.

It sounded like a lie, yet the Comanche language had popped out of his mouth. Judging from his dark hair and deeply suntanned skin, it was possible he was part Comanche himself.

"I'm going to join the rebel army," he said to Katherine. "What's your opinion?"

"About the war?" she said.

"About anything. Birds." Grinning, he pointed to swallows and scissor-tails darting about the yard.

Nautdah and Topsannah dozed on the porch. Nautdah. Like *naught*. Erasing who she was. It was the mating with the Indian that made her strange, Wesley understood. It was why Katherine scorned her.

"Look at those filthy hands," Katherine said.

"I rather look at you," said the cowboy. "What's your name?"

"You know what it is. Mrs. Parker."

"Tell me what it starts with."

She stood up. "You can sleep in the barn." She went in the house.

Next morning, while the cowboy washed up at the pump, Wesley said, "Leave Ma alone."

"She's not your real ma," the man said. "She told me."

"Just go," Wesley said.

"The friendly frontier." The cowboy dried his face on his sleeve.

He hung around all day, as if he had a right. In the evening, he and Katherine were back on the porch.

"You don't smile much," he said.

"Don't have reason to," she said.

"That squaw makes a lousy white woman, but you'd be a beautiful Indian."

Wesley held his breath.

"It starts with K," she said.

Inside, Nautdah worked at the spinning wheel. Wesley went to her and asked, "What does your name mean?"

Her mouth worked like a fish's. "Finded person."

It made sense. The whole world searched for Nautdah. She held up a huge hand, and he pressed his palm to it and felt her pulse beating. In her face, he found his father's blue eyes and wide jaw.

That night, he heard Katherine and the man together in the room next to his. They tried to be quiet in the bed where his father should be.

"Come to Mexico with me," the man said.

Wesley leaned closer to the wall.

"What about that war you're going to?" Katherine said.

They laughed and then remembered to be quiet.

✦ ✦ ✦

WESLEY felt short of breath, and he would wake up sweaty and hot. Katherine and the cowboy carried on like they were married. She quit taking Wesley to church. Nobody came out to visit, and there were no neighbors around to see what was going on, but Wesley saw, and Homer and Nautdah.

Then Homer vanished. Wesley searched the barn. Katherine said she ought to put a notice in the paper and put up signs in Canton, which was the nearest town, but she didn't. The cowboy did the work Wesley's father and Homer used to do—tending the sheep and cattle, feeding the horses, patching the roof. Wesley tried to help.

"You're weak. Scrawny. Feeble," the man jeered.

Wesley went to Nautdah. She'd become the person he sought out.

"Race you to the tree," he said.

She set Topsannah on the ground, beelined for a pin oak, and got there first. Panting, Wesley leaned over. She seized his face and looked into it, her hot leathery breath pouring over him.

"What?" he said.

She didn't answer, just took her hands away. Now she could run off, and he would let her, but she stayed.

✦   ✦   ✦

EVERY night, he listened at his bedroom wall.

"Have you heard from him?" the man said.

"No," said Katherine. "There ought to be a letter by now." After a long time, she said, "If I go, I can't come back."

"That's better," the man said. "I was watching you, before you ever saw me."

"How?"

"I saw you from far off, that hair of yours."

Wesley wondered what Katherine thought about that and if she liked it. She probably did. People were always praising her hair.

They were quiet.

"Don't," she said. "I just don't want to right now."

The cowboy said something.

"What'll we do when he comes back?" she said.

"*If* he comes back. That's why we got to leave."

Wesley thought he heard Katherine swallow. The wall was that thin.

He killed Pa. He was watching us, and he wanted her. The evidence tallied up in his mind: the cut on the man's arm when he first showed up. The bloody shirt. No letters from Pa. Homer must have figured it out. He must have run away, unless he was dead too, buried in soft earth inside the barn, or out on the prairie, black with flies.

✦ ✦ ✦

"SING," Nautdah said while Wesley chopped wood. Hard work, but he forced himself to keep at it. Was this how being a man would feel, the metal ache of joints, the thirst no water could quench?

"Sing like in wagon," Nautdah said.

Wesley set down the ax and stood straight. He sang "Camptown Races," his voice a breeze filling a sail. He sang "Gentle Annie" and "O! Susanna." Nautdah shaded her eyes with her arm as the sun climbed over the blackjack oaks. He sang "Lorena," "The Yellow Rose of Texas," and "Holy, Holy, Holy."

The singing gave him a plan. He would slip out at night, muster his strength for the twelve miles' walk to town, and tell people in Canton about the cowboy. Tell the preacher, the sheriff, the shopkeepers. Katherine would be angry, but the man would have to leave.

He sank down and laid his head on Nautdah's shoulder. He closed his eyes, and fever crept up his body. Her hand swept his forehead. She moved her ear to his chest.

"You die," she said. "Soon."

"No." His stomach tilted. He rolled aside and was sick on the grass.

"Nautdah die too," she said. "I eat now, for baby. Then stop."

"Don't," he said.

She pointed to the sky. "Sun tells. Pecos die of smallpox. Quanah live long. Strong man. My son."

✦ ✦ ✦

KATHERINE sought Wesley out while he fed the chickens.

"He talks crazy," she said. "I wish I'd never." She knelt, her hair draggling into the dirt. "I'm sorry, how I've acted to you."

"How come we don't hear from Pa?" he said.

A sharp kick in the rear knocked him sprawling. His teeth raked the dust. When he turned over, the cowboy towered above him, blocking out the sun.

Wesley struggled to his feet. "My pa'll kill you."

"He's in Virginia with buzzards eating his eyeballs," the man said.

"Go away," Katherine said. "Get away from us."

"You rather have him that can't tuh-tuh-talk? You tuh-tuh-told me he can't talk."

Wesley flew at him with his fists. Grinning, the man caught Wesley's arms and bent them behind his back, nearly out of the sockets. Wesley screamed from the pain.

Abruptly, the man collapsed, bringing Wesley down too. Chickens squawked and sprang high. Wesley squirmed out from under him, terrified and bewildered.

Nautdah loomed above them with a chunk of wood in her hands. She squatted beside the man, who lay splayed out, twitching and croaking like a bullfrog. Nautdah's eyes met Wesley's. She raised the wood and brought it down again and again on the man's face and chest until blood streamed and his teeth shot out, and the croaking and twitching stopped.

She dragged the body behind the chicken house. Katherine brought her a shovel and held Topsannah while Nautdah dug into the hard earth with strength, speed, and unflagging energy. Nobody told Wesley to go away, so he stayed. Katherine shifted the baby in her arms, undid her apron, and threw it over the pulped face, but Wesley couldn't stop thinking about the mashed eyes and the nose like raw liver. When the pit was deep enough, Nautdah pushed the body in, covered it with dirt, and beat the earth with the flat side of the shovel until the ground was smooth.

They took turns washing up at the pump, even Nautdah. Wesley drank the cold water like he'd never get enough. His head and face and hands were hot. He was hot all over, except for the water in his mouth.

A white moon hatched from darkness. He felt himself falling onto the grass and being lifted by his shoulders and ankles. The women were lifting him and talking, and the English words and the Indian words blurred together in his ears.

"Pa," he said. "I want Pa."

"I've got to get you to the doctor," Katherine said. "Hang on."

There was a jolting wagon ride, then a man reeking of whiskey and saying, "God almighty."

III

Katherine sold the livestock, left the farm, and lodged in town with Reverend Campbell and his wife Bessie. People treated her kindly, knowing her stepson had died and her husband was off at war.

"She lays in bed crying," Bessie Campbell told the neighbors. "I said, 'You've got a baby coming.' It was news to her, but I can always tell."

After a week, Katherine dragged herself into the Campbells' parlor, searched the hallways and kitchen, and looked out the windows.

"Where's Cynthia?" she asked. "Where's Topsannah?"

Bessie revealed that Reverend Campbell had dispatched mother and baby to Anderson County to live with Silas's younger sister, Orlena O'Quinn.

"He pinned the address to Cynthy's sleeve and put them on the train," Bessie said. "It's Orlena's turn."

Katherine surprised herself by saying, "I wish you'd asked me first."

Big, red-cheeked Bessie frowned. "Well, Orlena and me are friends since childhood. When I go visit her, you can come with me, if you want."

Katherine was distraught about being pregnant and fervently hoped the baby was Silas's. What if it wasn't? Obsessively, she counted backward the months and days. She had failed her husband, and she grieved for Wesley. He'd been a cute little boy—why hadn't she loved him till it was too late? She'd had him buried in town, in the churchyard. She was certain Silas was dead, murdered by the cowboy, and Homer too, and she was to blame. She couldn't stay with the Campbells forever, but her parents were dead and she didn't want to live by herself. She was in shock: the cowboy attacking Wesley, Nautdah bashing him to pieces, Wesley sick, dying, and dead. Of course, other than Topsannah, who was too young to take things in, and Nautdah, who had been banished, there weren't any witnesses to her love affair or the man's death. That was some consolation. Still she felt she was losing her mind. She wished she could talk with Nautdah about what had happened and what it all meant.

"Pray with me," she begged the Campbells.

Together the three of them knelt in the parlor, and she cried throughout devotions. Now she understood why Indian women hacked off their hair.

In the privacy of her room, she took out a pair of scissors. The mirror reflected her swollen, tearful face and cascading hair. Cautiously she snipped.

Bessie walked in and snatched the scissors away. "You're scared, is all."

"Who wouldn't be?"

"It'll be all right," Bessie said.

She had nursing and midwife experience, and that was a comfort. Katherine decided she would love the baby no matter whose it was, and nobody would know it wasn't Silas's.

Then the preacher started touching her during prayers: his hand on her back, his thigh against hers. She opened her eyes and edged away, but his long arm followed. She scooted till his arm waved in the air, but Bessie's eyes were open too. Only the preacher's eyes were still closed.

Bessie started picking on her, finding fault. Desperate, Katherine wrote to Isaac Parker. Could she stay with him and his wife?

Isaac welcomed her to Birdville, but his wife talked pointedly about unloved stepchildren in general and Wesley in particular.

"Quit makin' it worse," Isaac sighed.

When the baby came, Isaac's wife said, "He's got the Parker jawbone. He looks like *her*. The squaw, I mean."

Katherine agreed. She'd never felt so relieved in her life. She named the baby Luke.

✦ ✦ ✦

LUKE was two and a half years old and Katherine was hanging wash on the line the day Silas showed up wearing a shirt and trousers pieced together from the uniforms of captured Yankees.

"I thought you were dead," said Katherine, astonished. "You never wrote."

He kissed her, lifted her, and swung her around. "Yes, I did, honey. You didn't write back. I had to ask around to find you."

Isaac and his wife burst out of the house and caught him up in their arms, knocking over the clothes basket. Luke crawled through the laundry.

"Where's Wesley?" Silas asked. His stammer was gone. "And who's this little fellow?"

✦   ✦   ✦

HIS letters had gone to the farm in Van Zandt County. Katherine found them stuffed in the door when she and Silas returned. Every window in the house was broken out by tramps, varmints, or hail. Fences were busted, and critters nested in the cupboards.

Silas set to work. He'd lost a finger at Petersburg but claimed it didn't hurt. Katherine found pieces of the spinning wheel broken up for firewood. She swept out the ashes while Luke played underfoot. It felt so strange to be back in the place where those terrible things had happened, and she couldn't tell Silas about it. She pictured the cowboy's arm poking through the ground, his body heaved up by frost.

After they ate, she settled Luke on a pallet and slid into the musty, gritty bed with Silas. She shivered. At Uncle Isaac's, Silas had cried about Wesley.

"I did something bad," she blurted.

"Did you treat Wesley worse while I was gone than when I was here to see?" Silas's voice sounded rusty. "You never were kind to him."

"It was like you saw. I wish I'd been nicer." She gulped. "A man came here. I let him stay. I think he killed Homer. I was scared he'd killed you before you ever got out of the county."

Would he hit her? He never had, but she flinched from the hurt look on his face. She could see it even in the moonlight.

"You told me Homer ran off."

"He might've, but he might've been killed. I don't know."

"You were with another man, and Luke might be my son, or might be his. Is that what you're telling me?"

"He's yours. He favors you. People say so." In a rush, she said, "I got scared of that man. Nautdah killed him"—the first time she'd spoken the name, though she had thought of her as Nautdah for a long time.

"Cindy killed the man you laid with?"

"Yes, because he was hitting Wesley. She came up and conked him on the head. We buried him in the yard. Nobody knows."

She waited through the longest silence of their marriage.

"There was this woman," he said.

Was it relief she felt, that he had sinned too?

"When it was over," he said, "I thought about going back to her."

"Is she married? Where is she?"

"Tennessee," he said softly. "Ain't married."

Before he went to war, she was certain she could have done better, but now she loved him. "You can be free of me," she said, "if you rather be with her."

"I put her behind me," he said.

IV

The Texas legislature voted to give Cynthia Ann Parker a league of land and a pension of a hundred dollars a year for her suffering, but she never got the land or the money, because Texas decided the promises it made when it was part of the Confederacy didn't count, once it was forced back into the Union.

Silas sent money to Cynthia in care of Orlena, and Katherine suggested they visit, but Silas said the trip would be too expensive, and he didn't want to take time away from farming. He cursed the grasshoppers and drought, and season after season, they talked about leaving, but they couldn't decide where else to go.

Bessie Campbell's promised visits to Orlena did not take place, but Bessie corresponded with her and delighted in having news of Nautdah before Silas and Katherine did. Topsannah had died of fever, Bessie announced.

Katherine shivered, knowing how Nautdah had loved the child. Katherine feared more than anything that Luke would die. She and Silas wanted more children. Finally, when Luke was six, she had twins she named Matilda and Matthew.

At age two, they caught whooping cough. Katherine dosed them with licorice extract and barley water and had the doctor out, but their fevers didn't quit. Their faces grew pinched, and fear roiled Katherine's heart. It was March 1871.

Silas and eight-year-old Luke were out in the barn and Katherine was heating milk for the twins when a buggy jangled into the yard: Bessie Campbell.

"How do you stand this mud?" She eased into a kitchen chair, took off her bonnet, and fanned her florid face with it. "Worked up a sweat coming all the way from town." She set the bonnet down. "You look terrible."

"I've been up a few nights." Katherine nodded toward the twins, who were grizzling in their chairs. She didn't want to say how long they'd been sick. "Want some coffee?"

"Sure." Bessie loaded her cup with sugar. Katherine gave the children their milk and sat down. Bessie had to have news, to come all this way.

Bessie looked hard into her eyes. "Cynthy Ann is dead. Did you know?"

Katherine shook her head, but in that instant, she had guessed.

"Starved herself to death," Bessie said. "She caught the influenza, but she'd already quit eating. I had a letter from Orlena this morning."

"Starved . . . ?" It was too much to take in.

"How old was she?" Bessie asked.

Swiftly, Katherine calculated. "Ten years older than me. Forty-three."

"Where is Silas? Want me to tell him?" Bessie's eagerness was irksome.

"I'll tell him when he comes in for dinner. Have they had the funeral?"

"Oh my, yes. You don't leave a body laying around after influenza. They buried her in the graveyard in Poyner." Bessie's mouth flattened with satisfaction.

Katherine wiped milk from the twins' lips.

"Kinda puny," Bessie said. "All of mine were bigger at that age."

"They're getting over croup." Katherine adjusted the flannels around their necks.

"Hmm."

"Whooping cough," Katherine admitted.

"I knew it wasn't just croup," Bessie said. "Whooping cough can come back on 'em. You think they're on the mend, then here comes pneumonia."

Bessie put her palm on Matilda's forehead, then Matthew's. She had enough experience to tell if a child would recover. Or not. Katherine struggled to stay calm.

Bessie took her hand away. "The fever's broke. They'll be hungry."

Katherine let out her breath. She scrambled eggs in a skillet and fed them, and they ate with appetite.

"You been scared." Bessie's eyes narrowed. "You could've sent for me. I got powdered sea squills, best thing for cough." To the children, she said, "Next time, I'll bring some crayons. Would you like that?"

"Yes," they said shyly.

"Your hair's going gray, Katherine," Bessie said. "I didn't think it ever would. You used to be so preenified."

How could somebody be so maddening, even when they were helping you? Katherine's hands still trembled.

"What else did Orlena say about Nautdah?" she asked.

"Shoot, I been finding gray hairs since I was sixteen." Bessie held out her cup, and Katherine refilled it. "So it's Nautdah now? I don't recollect you calling her that. Orlena said she stayed furious-like, wanting to get back to the Comanches. And before she died, she had a vision."

"What do you mean?"

"She got all excited and called out *Quanah, Pecos*, like her boys was there in the room, then shut her eyes and gave up the ghost," Bessie said.

She picked up her bonnet and waggled it at Matilda and Matthew. Laughing, they grabbed the ribbons.

"Whatever she saw, it couldn't have been heaven, just the Great Spirit or some such," Bessie said. With a fingertip, she scraped sugar from the oilcloth and pressed it to the twins' lips. "Orlena told the newspapers, but they didn't print any death notice. Cynthy Ann used to be famous, and now nobody cares." Bessie hauled herself to her feet. "Tell Silas I'm sorry he lost his sister, even though she was trifling."

It was bait, but Katherine took it. "You don't have to be mean about her."

"Don't you care about Orlena? A burden's been lifted off her." Bessie opened the door, stepped out on the porch, and rounded on Katherine. "Get off your high horse," she sputtered. "You think you're the queen of the May. I came out here soon as I heard, to bring you news about your own family. You're welcome." She paused to see if the rebuke hit home.

"Thank you, and goodbye, Bessie." Katherine shut the door and leaned against it.

The twins looked at her. Color was coming back into their faces, and they kicked their heels against their chairs.

Matthew cocked his head. "Goodbye, Bessie," he said.

"Are you laughing or crying, Ma?" Matilda asked.

"I don't know." Katherine held the children tightly.

✦ ✦ ✦

WHEN Quanah Parker surrendered in 1875, leading the remnants of his people to Fort Sill, Oklahoma, Katherine wondered if that last march was the vision Nautdah had seen as she died—a splendid prophecy, her son triumphant even in defeat. Maybe the vision was Quanah's wolf-hunting jaunt with Teddy Roosevelt, or his success in the white world as a rancher and railroad owner.

Katherine became an ardent reader of newspapers, which eventually had a lot to say about Cynthia Ann Parker's life and death and repeatedly ran the old photograph of her nursing Topsannah. People wrote to the papers and claimed to be Topsannah or her descendants. Whites had taken her, lied to Nautdah that she was dead, and secretly raised her to adulthood.

Katherine didn't believe those articles but saved them along with the true ones. She expected a reporter to contact her or Silas, but time went by, and no one did. She considered writing about Nautdah herself but couldn't bear to. There was too much to tell, and she could certainly never write about the cowboy's death. The more she thought about it, Nautdah killing him wasn't the main story anyway.

The vision was.

In December 1910, when Katherine was seventy-two, she learned that Quanah had arranged for Nautdah's body to be moved to a cemetery in Cache, Oklahoma. Two months later, Quanah died and was buried next to his mother.

Was their reunion what Nautdah had foreseen? Was she finally at ease, maybe even joyful, in death?

Katherine knew how it felt to go from despair to ecstasy. She had feared her first baby was the cowboy's, and he turned out to be Silas's; had thought herself a widow, and Silas came home from the war; had believed the twins would die, and they'd made her a grandmother. Miracles every time. Luck was the difference between her life and Nautdah's, yet it was everything. Her whole selfish life, she'd been lucky.

She lifted the newspaper to the flyspecked kitchen window and squinted at the picture of Quanah, regal, clasping a feather fan. *A vision*: what came to mind was red-faced Bessie waving that bonnet while the twins played with the strings.

Fairy Tales

THE DRYER WAS BROKEN, and Mike O'Keefe had to do something about his wet clothes, so he strung ropes across the sunroom and draped his jeans, shirts, socks, and underwear over them. The zigzagging cords and dangling garments looked like sails and rigging. Way back in his family, there'd been sailors and whalers. He was proud of that. He wished he could show his creation to somebody, but he was alone, a hired hand at a house in Virginia, having driven down from Rhode Island to paint the roof. The owners, Jessica and Kurt Nelson, were at the beach. He'd been friends with Jessica for ten years, since high school, and now she'd married a very rich man. The house was Kurt's boyhood home.

It was October. Mike spent his days working. He liked being up as high as the crows and hawks in the fields, and calling the Nelsons from the rooftop: "It's going fine." The woods were pretty, with green among the red and gold. He'd never spent so much time alone. Neighbors down the hill, a young Mexican guy and an anxious-seeming woman, came over and borrowed a saw. Tulio and Sandy, their names were.

There was a church next door. One night he'd gone for a potluck supper and ate two helpings of everything, and the people were so nice, he stayed for gospel music and joke-telling. A man with a long white beard got up and did the scarecrow song, "If I Only Had a Brain."

That was Wednesday night. Now it was Saturday. Mike sat on the tiled floor of the sunroom with his wet laundry hanging over him. He drank melon seltzer while the sunset painted his socks and T-shirts pink. He'd been going to bed early and waking in pitch dark with mice mumbling in the walls.

Restless, he got in his pickup and drove to the nearest town, which was Culpeper. He found a country-and-western bar and ordered a beer. A dark-haired woman in glasses was dancing with two men, but she broke away from them and shimmied over. She was chunky but sexy in a short skirt and boots.

"Hey there," she said.

He shared his basket of nachos with her and told about working on the Nelsons' house.

"I know that place," she said. "There's a church next door."

"Yes." He described the potluck dinner and the man who sang the scarecrow song. He hummed it.

"Oh, don't." She covered her ears. "It gets on my mind." She laughed. "When will God come back? Jesus, I mean. He promised. It's been two thousand years." She waited, like she expected a real answer.

"What do you do for a living?" he asked.

"Teach third grade. I hate it. I'm going to quit at the end of the year."

The two men she'd been dancing with came over.

"Let's go," they said.

One of them leaned across Mike to grab her neck. Scary, a stranger reaching past him like that. The woman went with them, and they stumbled out the door.

"See ya," Mike called. He went out to his truck, planning to have a cigarette and go back into the bar, but instead, he fell asleep.

Early in the morning, his phone woke him up. His sister in Rhode Island.

"You'll be here tomorrow, right?" she said. "For the christening?"

Her baby daughter. He'd forgotten.

"I'm in Virginia on a job."

"You promised." She started to cry. "You're her godfather."

"All right, all right."

She'd had a rough time, lost her boyfriend, the baby's father, in a drowning accident. Mike sped back to the Nelsons' house for his ladders and tools and didn't feel too bad about leaving. He was almost done except for some of the flashing, and that could wait.

On the long drive back to Rhode Island, he thought about his sister's boyfriend. The guy had taken a five-year-old nephew out to look for bait and got caught on a sandbar with the tide coming in. Kept calling for help while the water rose past his ankles, to his knees, his waist. He put the kid on his shoulders, the ocean closing in: *It's up to my neck. Hurry.* Rescuers heard their cries but couldn't find them in the waves and fog. The bodies washed up the next day. His sister pregnant, hysterical, a wonder she didn't lose the baby. Hope, she'd named her.

✦   ✦   ✦

A local girl had gone missing, Marenna Steele, age nineteen. Six weeks had passed. Sandy Elder and Tulio Nunez sat at the table with the newspaper between them. There was a reward for information. Sandy didn't know the girl, but she'd memorized the facts. Marenna had told her mother she was going out to meet a new friend, and she'd never been seen again. Sandy felt sure if she and Tulio thought hard enough, they could solve the mystery, or at least come up with information to win the reward.

"What about that guy who was working over there? The roofer?" Tulio tilted his head toward the Nelsons' house.

Sandy's mouth popped open. "The guy from Rhode Island? We should have thought of him before. Didn't he leave around the time she went missing?"

"Let's go over," Tulio said.

They snatched up their coats and hurried out the door. They climbed the hill, slogging through the season's first snow. There was a steep place where Sandy had to stop and catch her breath. Tulio went ahead. So good-looking, he was, and so much younger. How would she ever hold on to him? She ran to catch up.

The Nelsons' house and its grounds were deserted, with *No Tres-passing* signs nailed on trees. Sandy fretted about leaving footprints. A swing creaked on the porch.

"That view." She swept her arm toward the Blue Ridge Mountains.

Tulio didn't answer. He was gathering sticks for their wood-burning stove. Sandy's little rental house was never warm. She had nothing, she was running out of time, she was forty-five and worked part-time at a day care, and didn't stand a chance if Tulio found some-body younger and prettier, and him with a restaurant job and chances left and right.

The reward would change everything.

Tulio hugged the firewood to his chest. "What are the owners like?"

She'd met Kurt and Jessica Nelson only once. "Rich. He's a lot older than her."

Tulio laughed. "Opposite of us."

Sandy decided she hated the Nelsons. Jessica Nelson would never have to work, and Tulio'd go nuts over her perfect face and jet-black hair. Snow seeped into Sandy's sneakers, and her hands itched misera-bly from the cold, because she'd lost her gloves.

They walked around the house.

"He didn't finish." Tulio pointed at the roof. "There ought to be metal at the bottom of that chimney."

They reached a corner that was all windows, like a greenhouse. Tulio set down his armload of wood and pressed his face to the glass.

"Look." He pulled her close.

Laundry sagged from makeshift clotheslines, rows of jeans and T-shirts and underwear, stiffly dried. Sandy gasped, and her eyes met Tulio's.

"It's his," she said, and he nodded.

Right there, she called the sheriff.

"That roofer guy left in such a hurry, when the girl went missing," she said. "He didn't finish the job, didn't even take his clothes. I'm look-ing at them." Tulio shook his head, and she knew she'd said too much, they were Trespassers, but the dispatcher just asked what the repair-man's name was. Sandy didn't know, "but you can call the Nelsons," liking the authority of saying that, even though the Nelsons wouldn't remember her from Adam.

All day, she and Tulio exulted. *Didn't even take his clothes.* That's the clincher, he said. You thought of him first, she said. You remembered the timing, he said. Timing was everything, they agreed.

✦   ✦   ✦

MIKE O'Keefe looked at the picture the cops from Virginia showed him. It wasn't the woman he'd met at the bar. The girl in the photograph— Marenna, they called her—was younger, and he'd never laid eyes on her. He said so. Through his kitchen window, he saw his pickup being towed away.

"Why did the Nelsons hire you, when you're all the way up here?" one cop said.

"Jessica knows my work is good."

"Why'd you leave in such a hurry?"

He told them about the christening.

"Are you willing to take a lie detector test?" they asked.

He was. That seemed to satisfy them, but they didn't make him take one, and they went away. A week later, he got his truck back. It smelled funny, like chemicals.

The woman he'd met in the bar: if anybody seemed like the type to go missing, it was her. He'd worried when the two guys hauled her out, but only for a second.

✦   ✦   ✦

JESSICA Nelson left Myrtle Beach over Kurt's protests, but Kurt was leaving, too, for Thailand. A venture capitalist, he traveled all the time. They'd been married so briefly, everything about him surprised her.

"That isolated house," he said. "Won't you be scared?"

His boyhood home in Virginia: he wanted to sell it, but after one visit, she'd loved it, the land and all the nature, and begged him not to. What a shock when the police had called. Would Kurt allow detectives to go into the house? Of course, he'd said. Volunteers would search the woods.

"One of us ought to be there," Jessica said.

"What if there's a killer on the loose?"

"That girl probably went to visit a boyfriend."

"Don't be naïve," Kurt said.

At least he'd believed her when she said Mike O'Keefe couldn't possibly have done it. Somebody was scapegoating him. The police must be running out of leads.

Kurt's cab honked, and he kissed her.

"Be safe," he said. "Buy whatever you need."

"I don't need much." She wasn't used to the money.

After he was gone, she packed up her car, locked the beach house, and made her way north and west across the Carolinas and deep into Virginia. When she reached the town of Culpeper, she stopped at a grocery store for supplies. *Missing* posters were taped to the doors, a photo of the girl, grinning. Jessica bought groceries, feeling she was back in her old, single life.

When she came out of the store, it was dark. On the sidewalk, people were singing and holding candles. A Christmas parade, she thought, until she saw the signs. *Marenna come home.* She drove slowly, afraid she'd hit somebody.

At the house, she found Mike's clothes strung up in the sunroom and had to laugh. It was the kind of thing he would do, ingenious and a little nutty. She'd expected to marry a guy like Mike instead of a tycoon twice her age. She'd met Kurt when she worked at the front desk of a swanky Providence hotel and he was checking in, all suntanned with expensive luggage.

"My God, it's Snow White," he'd said.

Now, alone in the house, she lay down in the narrow bed Mike had used. She was suddenly a stepmother, because Kurt had grown children she hadn't even met yet. The thought of them scared her. When she was by herself, she didn't feel married.

How dark it was, and what was that soft fumbling in the walls? She put out her hand and touched the cold plaster.

✦　✦　✦

ON Saturday, forty volunteers turned up, including a busload of Girl Scouts, to comb the woods behind the house.

"Go slow," a detective instructed, "and look for mounds or depressions in the earth." He glanced at Jessica. "We appreciate Mrs. Nelson letting us search her land."

She looked down at the ground, embarrassed at being pointed out. She was amazed so many people had come. She smelled damp earth, cedar, and melting snow. *Her land.* She had never owned any before. It was Kurt's, of course.

"Most of you know Angie Steele," the detective said.

A hard-faced, skinny woman stepped forward. "Bring my daughter back, y'all."

Jessica surprised herself by saying, "Was she a Girl Scout?"

"Don't say *was*," cried a man with a long white beard. "She's my granddaughter, and she is still alive."

"All right," said Jessica, taken aback.

"Mrs. Nelson," the man said, "I met your roofer at the church supper. A shady character."

"He had nothing to do with this," Jessica said. "I've known him all my life."

"Break it up," the detective said. "Everyone, go ahead and get started."

Jessica hadn't meant to be hooked into an argument. The accusations against Mike O'Keefe had shaken her, and she felt humiliated by the detective's scolding. Blindly, she glided past brush and briars, staying far away from the bearded grandfather. Don't be angry, she told herself, this is a tragedy, but she was boiling.

A tall young man fell into step with her.

"Would it be okay if I hunted deer here?" he said.

Well, these people were just full of surprises.

"I'll have to ask my husband." She should let Kurt handle everything. Look what happened when she took charge.

The bearded grandfather scuffed toward her through piles of leaves.

"When were you born, Mrs. Nelson?" he asked.

She stared at him. "Well, not yesterday."

The deer hunter snickered.

"Are you old enough to remember Patty Hearst?" the grandfather asked.

"No, but she was kidnapped, right?"

"It was 1974," he said. "The whole country got caught up in it. People kept thinking they saw her. My wife thought she saw her."

"I've got to go," Jessica said, but the old man reached out and grasped her sleeve.

"Patty Hearst was nineteen, Marenna's age," he said. "My wife kept saying, 'Patty Hearst was at the store, Patty Hearst was at the post office.' I'd say, 'Betsy, it wasn't her.' And she'd go, 'Oh yes it was, it was Patty Hearst,' and I'd go, 'Betsy, please.'"

"Wow," the hunter said.

"Our daughter Angie was just a baby then," the grandfather said, "and I figured my wife was strung out from being a new mom." In a falsetto, he said, "Patty Hearst was at the gas station."

"I'm so sorry." Jessica pulled away from him.

"What happened to her?" the hunter asked.

"She was found, perfectly okay," the old man said. "The bad guys kept her in a closet and made her shoot people."

"I mean what happened to your wife?" the hunter said. "What happened to Betsy?"

The grandfather glanced from him to Jessica. His eyebrows drew together slowly, and he edged away.

Puzzled, Jessica looked to the hunter.

"He's running," he whispered, watching the old man. "He actually ran away from us. Bizarre. What did I say? Did Betsy meet a bad end?"

Angie Steele broke away from a group of people and darted after the old man.

"Dad, hey," she called. "Dad, wait!"

The grandfather stumbled and fell, but he got up and limped toward the parked cars. Beside Jessica, the hunter made a strange humming sound. His body trembled, and a wheeze escaped from his lips.

"This is too much," he said. "Patty Hearst was at the store." He broke into snuffling laughter, doubled over, and echoed in a faint, creaky voice, "Dad, Dad."

Horrified, Jessica looked around and was relieved nobody appeared to notice him. She didn't want to be seen with him. When he gave way to another spasm, she slipped away and sought out the detective.

"Find anything?" she asked.

"No." The detective cupped a cigarette to his mouth.

"Mike O'Keefe isn't involved in this."

The detective clicked his lighter. "He's off the list. You can take down his laundry."

That was good news, at least. "So now what?"

"We've got some other leads. We're going to drag a lake." He looked at her hard. "What was so funny over there?"

The nerve. "Nothing."

The Scout leader blew a whistle, and girls swarmed back to the bus. Searchers shouted to each other, car doors slammed, and in moments, all the volunteers were gone, Angie Steele, her father, and the deer hunter too.

Jessica went into her house, ate an apple, and lay down for a nap, feeling she was under a spell. She couldn't sleep. She checked her phone. Kurt had texted. She wondered how a lake was dragged. She pondered Marenna's smile on the posters, triumphant, like she'd gotten away with something. And who was that deer hunter? His subversiveness was oddly appealing, but what a loose cannon, and anyway she was married—to a man she barely knew, on the other side of the world.

✦   ✦   ✦

SANDY wanted to join the search, but Tulio said it would be bad luck. All morning, they kept looking out the window. The house was cold. Sandy swept the ashes out of the woodstove and dumped them in the yard. In the distance, the searchers' jackets made bright spots of color in the Nelsons' forest.

Once the crowd had departed, Tulio went outside, looked around, and came back.

"No yellow tape," he said, "and the cops are gone."

"Maybe they're digging at the back of the woods," Sandy said.

"I went all around. They're done. They must not have found anything."

Sandy's heart sank. They'd been so sure. Ever since they'd found the guy's clothes, they'd been happy, even talking marriage. She couldn't bear to let go of that.

"The cops'll come back with bloodhounds," she said. "That guy did it. They'll pin it on him, wait and see."

"He's a long shot." Tulio'd given up.

"Oh, I'm not so sure about that. He might've chopped her up and stuck her in a crawl space." Memory struck her like a blow. She clapped her hands to her cheeks. "God, that saw we borrowed from him. Where is it?"

"Out on the woodpile."

She raced outside, grabbed the saw, and held it up. The metal teeth were full of wood shavings, "but blood spots can be so tiny," she said, "you'd need a microscope."

They argued. Throw it away, Tulio said, his fingerprints were on it now, hers too. No, she said, it might be the weapon, evidence, with the guy's DNA.

"He might have loaned it to us before he did anything, but he could've used it on other people," Sandy said.

"That's crazy talk."

"It ought to be tested."

"It'll only make *us* look bad." Tulio tore at his hair. "I'm sick of this."

"If I take it back to the Nelsons," she said, "I can find out if there's any news."

"You'll get us in trouble."

"We've got to do something, fast, or somebody else'll get the reward. I'll just go over and . . ."

"Leave them alone," Tulio shouted, his face as dark as a storm.

"Okay," she said, scared.

He left for work.

But she couldn't let go of her idea. He'd be gone till midnight. He wouldn't have to know. What could she take to the Nelsons, if not the saw? Anything, just to have an excuse to visit. She'd be nice, and she'd get them talking. She opened the cupboards and discovered a loaf of pumpkin bread, stale, but presentable once she sliced it and put it on a plate. And she needed something to prove she'd met what's-his-face, their handyman. Any old tool would do. She rummaged around and found a screwdriver.

She stumped up the hill, planning what to say. Her throat was dry, and her hand shook as she rang the doorbell.

Jessica Nelson answered, looking like she just woke up.

Sandy held out the screwdriver. "My husband borrowed this from your repairman." She offered the pumpkin bread. "And welcome back."

Jessica looked startled, but she smiled. "Oh, thank you." She took the things.

"We met before. I'm Sandy, from next door."

"Oh." Jessica obviously didn't remember her.

Sandy waited.

"Would you like to come in?" Jessica said. "I'm making coffee."

"Sure, just for a little while.

She followed Jessica. She'd expected the kitchen to be fixed up and fancy, but it was old-fashioned, almost as bad as her own. Jessica put a jar of instant coffee on a table and poured hot water into mugs. Sandy took a seat on a folding chair.

"Where's Kurt?" Saying his name easily, though she'd met him only the one time.

"He's in Thailand." Jessica sat down too.

"Wow, Thailand." Sandy stirred her coffee. She couldn't wait any longer. "All those people today—were they looking for Marenna Steele?"

"Yes, but they didn't find anything." Jessica sipped her coffee.

Sandy took a deep breath.

"I hate to tell you this, but your handyman acted weird, like he was hiding something. He didn't finish the job, did he? And he left out of here real fast."

Jessica looked her square in the eye. "He had nothing to do with it."

"Maybe not," Sandy said, like she knew otherwise. She'd made Jessica a little bit mad, and she felt an odd pleasure about that.

"Thailand," she said. "Isn't that where people go for plastic surgery?" She'd seen it on TV. "You can have a face-lift plus a vacation."

Jessica's mouth went tight.

"What if Kurt comes back like this?" Sandy sucked in her cheeks and stretched her eyes with her fingers, "with the little bitty pixie ears? They do the ears too."

Jessica set her mug down with a thud, but Sandy couldn't stop.

"A friend of mine married this guy she thought was rich," she said, riffing, making it up, "and he got a face-lift, and it turned out all creepy." She made a goofy expression, squinting and lolling her tongue. "And soon he was asking *her* for money. He didn't have a dime. And she divorced him."

Where had all that come from?

"That's too bad," Jessica said, really mad now.

So Sandy had to act polite. "Do you need anything? I've got an extra thing of fish sticks. I can run over and get them."

"No thanks." Jessica stood up. "I have a lot to do."

Sandy'd gone too far. She'd backtrack a little.

"So that friend of mine, she went online and met this guy that sounded wonderful, and everybody said watch out, he's too good to be true, but he turned out to be fantastic. For real." She was out of breath.

Jessica glared.

"Happily ever after," Sandy said.

"Well," Jessica said, "that's nice," and Sandy knew she'd blown it. Jessica would never talk to her again.

Jessica led the way down the hall. The bum's rush. Sandy's anger soared.

At the door, Jessica said, "Wouldn't it be nice if Marenna was home for Christmas?"

"She's dead. Everybody knows it."

"There's always hope."

"Oh, baloney. Somebody killed her and threw her away like a piece of shit."

They stared at each other. Yes, Tulio would think Jessica was beautiful. Black hair and real pale skin. Sandy wanted to slap her. She clenched her fists.

"Please go," Jessica said.

Somehow Sandy got through the door. Her head spun. Her feet carried her down the porch steps and away. So she'd told off Jessica Nelson. She'd gone over to be nice and friendly, and it had gone all wrong, but it wasn't her fault. She was just being neighborly, and Jessica'd thrown her out.

If Tulio knew, he'd pitch a fit.

But that bit about the face-lift? Oh, give herself credit, that was great. Did she dare act it out for him? Maybe she could make him laugh. Put all this in perspective. Show him she could bounce back. They'd bounce back together.

The sun had set. The sky burned with colors, green and purple and pink smeared above the dark humps of the mountains. It was very cold. Snow glimmered under her feet.

Darn it, she'd burned her tongue on the coffee. She swallowed, and it wasn't just the coffee. The back of her throat felt scratchy in a sick way. She stopped on the steep part of the hill and swallowed again. Yes, she was getting a sore throat. Maddening, the colds she caught at the day care, and the older she got, the longer it took to get well. She might be sick all through Christmas.

The giddy feeling evaporated, and what remained was truth as sharp as winter air. It was just a fairy tale to think she could hang on to Tulio. She would always be poor, and he would leave her, and she'd be stuck forever in that lonely, dumpy house.

The happiest moment of her life was when they found those clothes. She'd relived it a thousand times, the way he pulled her to him and said, *Look.* There was the laundry, wild and crazy on those ropes. Jackpot. On that patio in the snow, she'd been so close to luck and money.

There must be other clues.

In the woods? No harm in looking. If she didn't find Marenna Steele, maybe she'd hit on some treasure, the way relic hunters found bullets and buckles and such, and didn't farmers dig up jars of gold coins in their own fields? Maybe one of the searchers had dropped a big fat billfold stuffed with cash.

She cut across the hill and went the long way behind the house, so Jessica wouldn't see her, and entered the forest. Thorns pricked her hands, and she smelled evergreens. This was like the stories she read to her day-care kids. You'd go into the woods, and your life would change. She pushed through a tunnel of briars until she reached a clearing where the tree trunks were massive and spaced apart. The branches had woven a canopy overhead.

She knelt down and brushed at pine needles. It was almost too dark to see, and very quiet, and she listened closely in case somebody tried to sneak up. Her fingers grew sticky with sap and so cold she could hardly flex them, but she kept raking the ground.

If Jessica came out and wanted to know what she was doing, she'd say, "Oh, I lost something here a long time ago."

"What was it?" Jessica would ask.

Sandy'd be ready for that. A person could lose anything in the woods.

"A ring," she'd say, "I lost a ring."

Or a bracelet, or a watch, or the heel of a shoe.

Interview with Etta Place,
Sweetheart of the Sundance Kid

San Francisco, California
June 1970

Newspapers have me dead twice already—burned up in a house fire and shot by a lover, but I got out of the flames in time, and the bullet missed. The fire was here, and the shooting was in Argentina. Been stalked by the reaper since I was born, in 1878, a yellow fever year.

I *disappeared into the pages of history,* yet here I am, ninety-two. But you want to learn about Sundance. Harry Longabaugh.

For the longest time, the Pinkertons was after Harry and me. There was one fella who asked to be taken off train duty so he could hunt for me full time. A woman likes being chased. Detective or sweetheart don't make much difference. The U.S. marshals hounded us too, and private-eye types hired by Wells Fargo and the banks—spies or cops or whatever you want to call them. Thugs, mostly.

Frank Smith, H. A. Brown, Harry A. Place, Harry Long. Those were Harry's other names. Alias Sundance.

You might say Harry and me was in demand.

BUTCH CASSIDY

He was horrible. Write that down. Said he'd tried to please everybody all his life, and all it got him was mad. He picked his nose—with two fingers. Never mind what you've heard, I was never his girl. I wouldn't even touch his sleeve. He and Harry were not as loyal to each other as you might think. George LeRoy Parker was his real name. It took Harry's image down, to associate with the likes of him. I told him so.

HOW IT ALL BEGAN

With tapeworms. Harry got hold of big ones at a stockyard and put them in jars. The day I met him, he was with a medicine show. Harry's boss wore a feather headdress. Harry had on a nice suit he'd bought from an undertaker, and he was the one who took the money, telling folks what a bargain they were getting, saying he himself had passed a tapeworm the size of an eel. Sometimes he'd point to a particular jar and say that one was his. People loved it.

So how did we meet? It was June 1897, in Belle Fourche, South Dakota, and I was nineteen. My ma sent me to buy whatever medicine was for sale. I rode a mule three miles from my family's farm, wearing a bonnet to keep the sun off my face. The medicine wagon was parked at the square. Money and bottles of Kiowa Kure-All Pills changed hands as fast as customers could shove dollar bills at the man in the nice suit: Harry. Harry's boss was one fast-talking fake Indian. His headdress wagged up and down. Feathers fell off, and youngsters stuck them in their hair. A man pulled up and started selling bottles of beer, "to wash the pills down with, don't wait till you get home, get better right this minute." They were all in cahoots, beer seller and white Indian and good-looking young fella in the suit.

When Harry and I saw each other, the medicine show and the whole Wild West just flat disappeared. His blue eyes locked on my face. Fifty people in that crowd, but he picked me out with a look, and in that instant, I didn't hear anything, didn't see anything except him, all strong shoulders and white teeth and the sun on his hair. People mobbed him. I thought of a lighthouse on a rocky island. Waves crashed against the rocks, but the lighthouse stood tall and shining. I let my bonnet fall back so he could see my face.

His boss said, "You seem to have hypnotized my assistant."

Everybody laughed, and Harry laughed without taking his eyes off mine. He was choosing me, and it's a wonderful feeling, being chosen. I stuck out my hand with Ma's dollar in it, and the crowd parted. Harry was Moses strolling through the Red Sea. He gave me a bottle of pills and folded his hands over mine, and his smile went up into his eyes.

"Wait for me," he said.

"I will," I said, before we even knew each other's names.

When the crowd thinned out, the boss whipped off his headdress and skedaddled into a saloon.

"Harry Longabaugh, at your service," Harry said and bowed. His hat fell off, and a little boy caught it and sailed it to him. He dusted it against his knee. "I saw you riding into town from a mile off."

It was a gift, he said. Other people needed field glasses to see as well as he could. Made him a good hunter and a good shot.

"I'm buying this stuff for my ma," I said. "I'm not sick."

He held my mule by the bridle and said, "I'll tell you a secret."

Kiowa Kure-All Pills were nothing but little strings, he said, rolled up tight and covered with sugar paste. People swallowed the pills and passed the strings and thought it was goodbye, tapeworm.

"I want my money back," I said.

"All right." He handed me a dollar. "Now I've made a bad impression. Can I make up for it?"

"How?" I said.

"Wait here." Harry snapped down the canvas flap on the medicine wagon, went into the general store, and came out with a bunch of yellow bananas and a sack of oranges. He skinned a banana and fed it to my mule. I peeled an orange and ate it, piece by piece. It was sweet and cool. It took the dust out of my mouth.

Last week, a girl came out here from a college to talk to me, and when I told her about the fruit, she said, "Just like the Garden of Eden. Adam and Eve. That'll be my . . ." and she used a long funny word for homework.

Yes, I've seen the movie. They got some things right. It shows what I felt for Harry. But they got Butch all wrong, and I never rode a bicycle with him. I went to see the movie with my great-granddaughter, Barbie. She cried at the end, and when we went out in the lobby, she yelled, "This is her. Etta. My great-grammaw," but nobody paid any attention to us.

So Harry gave me bananas and oranges.

"Tell your mother this'll do her more good than pills," he said.

"Tell her yourself."

"Sounds like an invitation," he said. "I accept."

So he came out to the farm with me. Ma liked him, but she couldn't keep a secret. She blabbed the truth about the tapeworm pills to friends and neighbors, and soon Harry got fired and was looking for another job. I said, "Why not rob a bank?"

I'd said it to others. He was the first one who saw I meant it.

WHAT SHE KNOWS OF SUNDANCE'S HISTORY

Born in Pennsylvania in 1867 and ran away from home at sixteen. Stole a horse and spent eighteen months in Sundance, Wyoming, only time he was in jail. He nicknamed his own self. Got out of jail, went up to Calgary, and worked as a cowhand. In 1892, he robbed a train in Montana. Claimed he didn't steal another thing until I suggested it.

We slept together in my room. Ma could see I loved him, and Pa and my brother were gone to the gold fields. Harry found out I liked Indian names. He'd say them so each name made a whole world. "Gall. Red Cloud. Young Man Afraid of His Horses." He'd say a name and kiss me, and then, well.

By then, the Indians was tame. Sitting Bull had been in Buffalo Bill's Wild West Show. People paid to see him ride a horse and shoot a gun, and they clapped when his long braids flew around. By 1890, he was an Indian for real again, dancing the Ghost Dance and trying to save what was left of the Sioux. I was just a little girl when he was shot at the Standing Rock Agency.

Back to me and Harry. June 28, 1897, was so hot, the wash dried on the line before I got it all hung. A boy came galloping out to the farm with a note from Harry. He'd robbed the Butte County Bank with four of his friends.

For three years, I didn't see him. He wrote me, though. *Wait for me, Etta.* He hid in Utah with Elza Lay and the Wild Bunch. When other men came to see me, talking marriage—even the head of the Butte County Bank, I'm not making that up—it was easy to turn 'em down. I was in long-distance love. I stayed on the farm with Ma. Tended the chickens. Taught a hen to ride on a dog's back. Called 'em my Wild Bunch.

Thought you'd appreciate that. Your nose wrinkles when you laugh. How old are you, anyway?

WHY IT WASN'T JUST ANY LOVE STORY

Because of the ranch. Ever been to Argentina? Big sprawling grasslands, moon over jagged mountains. Steak every night. Everything smells better there, even fire. Cowboys with banjoes and all of them working for us, raising cattle.

Women that run with outlaws, they tend to be common. Pearl Starr. Have you ever seen a picture of her? And Bonnie, that went with Clyde? Harry would never've gone for them. He said I had refinement.

So the ranch, and me, made him different. It was the sweet look I had in the one picture of us, yes, that one. Harry bought that watch for me at Tiffany's, and Mr. Tiffany himself pinned it on my blouse. I've still got it, and it still keeps good time.

Speaking of pictures, here's Percy, my son, and this is Barbie, my great-granddaughter that took me to the movie. Percy's father owned a grocery store in Oregon. I was married to him for thirty years. So, no, Percy and Barbie aren't any kin to Harry.

MARRIAGE TO SUNDANCE

In 1900, Harry robbed a bank in Nevada, struck it rich, and sent for me. I went by train to St. Louis. He had a preacher lined up. We said the *I do's* and went out for fried chicken. The fly in the ointment was Butch, and the federal marshals that were after him and Harry. That was why we left the country.

On the boat going down to South America, Butch was seasick, and I had to tend to him. Harry and I talked about having babies, but I said, "We've already got a child, a thirty-four-year-old baby." Harry laughed, but I was mad.

Life got better. Harry and Butch bought that beautiful piece of Argentina and put my name on the deed, too. Seven, almost eight, years I had with Harry. That's all I'll say. Some things, a person likes to keep private.

DEATH OF SUNDANCE

A gun battle with soldiers in San Vincente, Bolivia, in 1908, is the official story. Butch and Sundance, blown to smithereens. That's what people want to believe.

But talk to Butch's sister, Lula Parker Betenson. She's a state senator from Piute County, Utah, and she'll tell you Butch was alive and well at a family reunion in 1925. He'd been trapping and prospecting. Died in Spokane, Washington, in 1937. Lula talks to the papers all the time. Sometimes she claims he went to Europe, or he ran for governor under a different name.

Harry? Some say he got killed in Uruguay in 1911 while robbing another bank. Or retired to Casper, Wyoming, called square dances till his voice gave out, and died of old age about 1936.

There may be graves in San Vincente, Bolivia, but the bodies aren't Harry and Butch. There's many miles and many tongues between Bolivia and the rest of the world, twisting up the truth.

The real story is this. Are you ready?

Harry and Butch never left the ranch in Argentina. Pals don't always stay on good terms. Things had been so nice. We'd made friends with other ranchers. One of the wives offered to teach me piano. So Harry sent to Buenos Aires for a baby grand. The day it came, I was so excited. Big and beautiful, it was, of mahogany wood with a top that lifted up, and a swerve in its side. I sat down on the bench and drew my fingers up and down the keys, set my feet on the pedals, and songs came out. Real music. The ranch hands heard it, and the neighbors. My songs carried on the wind, and soon a crowd filled the house—a party, with food. Beer. Dancing. Every time I touched those keys, music came out, like in a dream. I didn't need even one lesson.

Butch got drunk and picked a fight about where the piano ought to go.

"It stays here by the window," I said.

Butch didn't want it there, and he shoved it so hard it smashed into a wall. Talk about the Hole-in-the-Wall gang. Harry drew his gun, and so did Butch, and they shot each other faster than you could say middle C. The neighbors screamed and stampeded, jumped on horses, and were gone.

Party over, and my husband and his trouble-making friend, dead.

The ranch hands dug the graves. The foreman, Juan Miguel, read from the Bible. Psalms sound pretty in Spanish. At sunset, I brought out a lantern, and he kept on reading.

Harry left me enough money to pay the taxes for two years. That was two years I didn't laugh or cry. I put flowers on Harry's grave, such as bloomed on those high plains. The days of steaks and banjoes was over. I was a widow, with my beauty froze over, and gray coming into my hair.

WHAT BECAME OF THE RANCH

That foreman, Juan Miguel, I liked. I let him live in the house. We weren't married. He was the one who took a shot at me. How did the newspapers get hold of that, enough to get it almost right, when nobody knew about the piano party?

Juan Miguel said, "Etta, stick this feather on your hat"—it was from a condor, great big bird of the Andes—"and I'll aim for it."

I was packing my trunk to go back to the States. It was just time to go, was how I felt. I put the feather on my hat and stood up straight. Would Juan Miguel kill me? I almost didn't care. He plugged the feather, ruined the hat. I clapped the trunk shut, and he hauled it to the wagon and drove me to the train depot. It was a long way on a narrow road. A horse could lose footing and slide down the mountainside.

What if Juan Miguel was the man I was meant to be with? A part-Indian cowboy with skin like saddle leather, and easy with a rope?

He could make a lasso sing, keep a rope humming in a circle above his head, then bring it down around a bull's neck. He loved me enough to cry when I left, but I didn't even look back. Somebody else must be living there now. You could go. Ask around till you found it. I'm done talking about it. It hurts too much. Ask me something else.

WHAT ETTA WANTS PEOPLE TO KNOW

When my son Percy was ten years old and had the mumps, I remembered the trick about a chicken riding on a dog. I told Percy to go to his window, and I went out in the yard and put a rooster on a hound's back. The rooster kept falling off. After a few tries, it stuck. Percy's face lit up, and he laughed, and soon he was well again. Percy's father ran a grocery store in Oregon. I told you that. Sure I helped. Weighed cheese, counted nails. The customers saw the rooster riding the dog, and they loved it. Best show in town, especially for Oregon in the nineteen-teens.

Of course my kinfolks know my real name. Barbie tells everybody she meets, and her mother told her sewing circle, but nobody believes 'em. Barbie and me are more like friends than relations, never mind the age difference. She took me to a peace rally at Golden Gate Park. We ate snow cones and talked with tourists.

Why San Francisco? Why not? You can live cheap with a hot plate and a shared bathroom. There's Chinese markets close enough to walk to. I'm lucky. Not every landlord'll let you keep cats. There's a new one I want to catch.

Here, take this bowl, and help me get my coat on.

SIDESTEPPED BY HISTORY?

Bend down and look under the cars. It's got a white nose. No, my name in the phone book's not Place. You know that. But say Etta Place in the story. It still feels right.

What if the star was me? If they made a show about my own real life? The girl that took Harry from tapeworms to Hollywood.

I see it. Here kitty, kitty, come here.

Put the bowl down so he'll smell the milk.

There, kitty, that tastes good, don't it?

Say I'm wearing one of those ruffled white dresses, with my hair piled up and my skin still creamy. Say I've got some secret that keeps me beautiful, like the girl in the movie. Write it with me in the middle, not off to the side.

Keep the scene where Harry and Butch rush out of hiding, and everything freezes. You hear all that gunfire, and you know they'll die. I can see why people like that part. It builds up and builds up, with fighting and music, and they're bleeding and hurt but still cracking jokes, and no way out except through that door, surrounded by police, turning into heroes before your very eyes.

My great-granddaughter cried. She couldn't stop, even when I told her it wasn't like that. She grabbed my hand and held on, like I could go back and change things.

Ghost Walk

September 1899
Philadelphia, Pennsylvania

In the basement of a stone house in Chestnut Hill, seventeen-year-old Frances Watkins and her mother are treated to a tour of an unusual collection, a group of preserved bodies owned by Vaughan Beverly, the widowed Mrs. Watkins's fiancé.

Vaughan gestures to a glass-topped casket. "This woman turned to soap."

Frances feels sick. The dinner at the restaurant where Vaughan took them was rich and heavy, and she drank too much champagne. She wishes her mother had never met Vaughan Beverly on his mysterious trips to Baltimore, where Frances and her mother used to reside. Tomorrow her mother will marry him, and they will all live in this house, in one of Philadelphia's most luxurious neighborhoods.

I won't stay here, Frances vows. She and her mother have known about the dead people in the basement. Vaughan boasted of them at the party where Frances and her mother first met him, at the home of wealthy relatives. Vaughan is a man of science, everyone says.

Yet to see the corpses in person is a shock.

Her mother acts as if it's a grand joke. Maybe after the wedding, she'll come to her senses and have the bodies taken away. Surely it is wrong to have them here, as if they are of no more consequence than Vaughan's display cases of butterflies and beetles, with their carefully printed labels. He collects many things—guns, knives, and trophies of exotic animals. Last night, Frances stayed up late in his extraordinary library, reading about birds.

The basement is furnished as beautifully as the rest of the house, with electric lights, upholstered couches, and paintings on the walls.

As for the cadavers, Frances can't help but be intrigued.

"Turned to soap?" she asks, peering through the glass. The woman is naked except for strips of cloth over her breasts and loins, and her skin appears whitish-gray.

"Tell us more," says Mrs. Watkins. She sips from a glass of wine and places a hand on Vaughan's arm.

"She came from an old cemetery by the river," Vaughan says. "Being rather rotund, well, her fat combined with chemicals in the wet earth. The substance is called adipocere. It's like lye soap."

"Adipocere," says Mrs. Watkins. "It sounds French. *Adipocere!*" She waves her hand.

"How do you know she's soap?" Frances asks. She imagines Vaughan in a bathtub, humming and lathering. She heard him humming last night, while she searched for towels in a cupboard outside his lavatory. It's strange that in a house so ornate and well-appointed, there don't seem to be any servants.

"I have washed with her," Vaughan says. "If you mix a bit of her with some crushed lavender, it's the finest soap you'll ever have. I'll open the case so you can pinch off a piece."

"Oh, no, that's all right," Frances says.

She feels light-headed, and she assumes it's from the company of the dead. Vaughan's collection includes a pickled baby floating in formaldehyde, three adult mummies, and a remarkably fresh-looking boy about Frances's age.

Vaughan thumps the glass cover of the casket holding the boy.

"The Young Master was almost certainly a Revolutionary War soldier," he says. "He turned up near the site of an old hospital."

"Turned up?" asks Frances, determined to challenge him. "Did you dig for him?"

"He was brought to me already embalmed. I had this uniform made for him."

"Does the constable know these people are here?" Frances says.

"The authorities have enjoyed this same tour." Vaughan points to a table in corner. "We play poker with the soap lady and the Young Master looking on."

Frances turns away. She shouldn't have goaded him. In a moment, fingertips touch her back, just the lightest pressure. She has experienced the sensation before and assumed it was an accident. Does her mother see? No, she is absorbed with the Young Master.

Frances returns to the soap woman and gazes at the mute face, the webbed-looking eyes, and the dark pit of the slightly open lips. The glass is cloudy over the mouth, as if the body breathes now and again. Frances marvels: to think that this woman lived and spoke and ate, perhaps loved a man and bore children. And her body, without her soul in it, wound up at this mansion in the northwestern part of the City of Brotherly Love.

For the past three days, Vaughan has entertained Frances and her mother. They rode in his carriage through the leafy avenues of this exclusive neighborhood, with Vaughan calling out the names of streets in a clarion voice: "Shawnee Street. Mermaid Lane." They explored the cool splendor of Fairmount Park. Vaughan's horses pulled to the edge of a ravine, and Frances held her breath as they gazed into Wissahickon Gorge.

It is the end of summer, the last year of the century. She feels nostalgic and keenly alert.

Today they took the trolley down Germantown Avenue. It went faster than she had ever moved before, flying over the Belgian-block cobblestones of the swerving street while pedestrians ran pell-mell out of the way. Passengers held their hats during the steep careening slide. Vaughan pointed out great houses that belonged to friends of his, where, he said, he and Frances and her mother would soon dine and dance, and Frances would meet young people who would be congenial, he promised. Frances couldn't help but thrill to the thought, even though she has decided she must run away from Vaughan's house, away from these bodies that he waited until tonight to show them, as a *pièce de résistance.*

She and her mother are being saved by Vaughan, and all three of them know it, saved from a wretched district of Baltimore where ragged laundry flaps on lines and the streets smell of garbage. Frances's mother has never allowed Vaughan to visit them there; in the three months they have known him, he has courted her mother in the homes of more prosperous Watkins relations. Frances can't remember her father, who died when she was young. She feels like an old woman, as if she and her mother have switched places. It should be Frances who has won the prince, she and not her mother marrying the strange, compelling Vaughan Beverly.

Yes, Frances is in love with him, she admits as she regards the soap woman's ravaged face. She keeps a tiny photograph of him in a locket around her neck, and when she is alone, she examines it, admiring his dark golden eyes, Roman nose, high cheekbones, and the slight puffiness of his lips. In her fantasies, something happens to her mother—oh, not anything bad, but something clean and painless that simply takes her mother away—and then he falls in love with her, and they live happily ever after in this cavernous house on West Evergreen Avenue, and when she steps into this basement as Mrs. Vaughan Beverly, it's like any other basement, holding only damp bricks and piles of ashes. She would not give herself to him until they were actually married—unlike her mother, who has occupied his bedroom these past three nights. It wasn't only Vaughan humming in the lavatory last night, it was her mother too. In the mornings, the three of them have breakfasted together in the enormous kitchen. Vaughan scrambles eggs in a great iron skillet and pulls thick slices of toast from a blazing oven. Maybe there are servants after all, because Frances never sees a dirty dish from one morning to the next.

She consults the soap woman silently: *Can it be? Will I be with him?* The glass of the casket fogs a little, but it's Frances's breath. She takes out her handkerchief and rubs at the spot. How can she possibly long to stay with him, and yet know that she must run away? Where will she go? Back to Baltimore? No. She's in a new place, Chestnut Hill. The name rings in her mind like a bell. *When I was seventeen, I came to Chestnut Hill,* she imagines telling the soap woman. Then the story in her head stops, because she can't conceive of what might be next. Probably nothing will ever happen to her, and she will always be her same plump self, with freckles.

Her mother and Vaughan are kissing.

"But why?" Frances asks. "Why would someone bring you a dead body? Why would you take it, and why do you have so many?"

"Francie," her mother says, from within the circle of Vaughan's arms. "He's a man of science."

Science seems to represent all that Frances will never understand. She bursts into tears.

"Would it make you happy, Frances," Vaughan asks, "if I buried them?"

Frances stares at him. Will it be this easy? To object, to cry, and then to get her way?

"There's no need," her mother says, but Vaughan lifts a hand to silence her.

"Yes," Frances says.

Vaughan looks from Frances to her mother. "Then they shall be buried."

Frances's tears dry on her cheeks. *Her face was wreathed in smiles*— she read that line somewhere, and it comes back to her as she beams at Vaughan, then drops her gaze, abashed.

Her mother is scowling. "Any objection to the dead butterflies, Frances?"

"No."

What has come over her mother? This woman in the lacy white dress—*Thank heavens for this dress,* her mother confided during the courtship; *one nice dress and my good complexion.* Is this the same woman who struggled to keep their house clean, sewed clothing for the rich relatives, and made Frances say her prayers every night?

"The dead people can go to a museum, Vaughan," her mother says. "Aren't they valuable?"

"Yes, and I'll miss them." Vaughan strolls over to Frances. He taps the soap woman's casket. "This one, of course, we could just use up."

"Keep her, at least," Frances's mother says.

"No, I've had their acquaintance long enough. I'll see that each one is decently interred."

"Thank you," Frances says. Generosity has always embarrassed her. "If you'll excuse me, I think I'll go to bed."

"Of course," her mother says coldly, and Vaughan nods.

Frances pauses. Something else is amiss, aside from a basement full of bodies. With a wedding tomorrow, shouldn't there be neighbors and friends calling to wish them well? Vaughan has lived in Philadelphia all his life. Where is his family? He is not old; he is possibly younger than her mother. Is he alone in the world? *The authorities* are the only people he has mentioned coming to his house, to play poker. She is overcome by the conviction that the wedding will not take place, that this is all some ruse.

"Well, goodnight."

She hurries out of the basement and up the stairs, down a deeply carpeted hallway, and up another staircase. At last she reaches the guest room, with its high feather bed and cheval mirror.

She opens the mullioned windows and breathes the scent of pine and spruce. The window overlooks a dark, terraced garden. There is a boxwood maze, and winding paths marked with urns and statuary, and a deep still pool with pink waterlilies and gliding goldfish. The first morning, Vaughan led Frances and her mother on a tour, while her mother pawed at him in the most embarrassing way.

Well, if Frances stays—and what else can she do?—the garden will offer solace. She pictures herself reading beneath a latticework trellis and looking up from her book in hopes that Vaughan might be nearby.

The nighttime emits a glow. Tree frogs are cheeping, and low throaty croaks issue from an unseen animal or a bird of prey. Their songs and cries are old familiar ones of summer ending and autumn beginning.

She is alone, like the soap woman. She has no friend to tell her fears to, no one to write a letter to. Since leaving school two years ago, she has kept company only with her mother, assisting with the sewing that has provided a subsistence living, and anticipating and dreading the invitations from relatives. She and her mother went forth bravely, in hopes someone like Vaughan would rescue them. Donning the lace dress, her mother had asked in anguish, *How many times must we do this?*

"And here I am," says a voice behind her.

Frances whirls. There stands Vaughan. In the light of the wall sconce, he looks taller than ever, his face ruddy, his hair golden, and his brow smooth.

"May I sit down?"

He eases into a slipper chair, but she remains awkwardly on her feet. She finds herself wondering whose room this used to be, who chose the rose-colored damask for the chair and whose face has been reflected in the mirror. Vaughan glances into it and straightens his collar.

Why is he here? Has she done something wrong?

"You're scared," he says. "How can I set your mind at ease?"

"Do you love my mother?"

"I love you, Frances. You knew tonight. Didn't you?"

She has longed to hear these words, yet she feels only alarm. He rises from the chair and takes her hand. His fingers are warm and strong.

"It's not too late," he says. "You and I can be married."

"What about Mother? Would she live here with us?" Frances's head is spinning. She can't believe they are saying these things.

"I've been trying to figure it out. Things have moved rather fast. And just now, I'm sorry to say . . ." His voice trails off.

"What?" Frances pulls her hand out of his grasp. "What do you mean? Where's Mother?"

He regards her with an expression of great gravity. After a pause, he speaks softly and urgently. A few moments ago, it seems, her mother said she felt ill, and she clutched at her heart and collapsed.

"She seemed to recover a little, and rose up and kind of staggered. She got as far as the Young Master, and then she, well, died. She's dead."

Terror ripples along Frances's spine. She tries to scream, but only a sigh comes out. Vaughan settles onto the slipper chair and tugs her into his lap. His midsection feels doughy, pressing against her hip. He caresses the back of her neck with the light, stinging touch she recognizes.

She looks into his golden eyes, mere inches away. He can't possibly have said what she thinks he said.

"I've got to go to her." She tries to get up, but he pulls her back into his lap.

"A young woman and her mother travel north," he says. "The mother is to marry a scientist. On the eve of her wedding, she suddenly perishes. The man marries the lovely, innocent daughter instead. It's just as well, since he'd begun to find the mother tiresome, with a ghoulish streak."

"She was angry with me," Frances murmurs. "This wouldn't have happened if I hadn't made her mad."

"You wanted to do the decent thing. Bury those bodies. A man wants a woman who'll make him do the proper thing."

"Is this a joke?"

"This house knows no jokes."

She flings his hands away, leaps up, and runs out of the room. She hurtles down the stairs and into the basement. A still figure is splayed out on the floor.

"Mother." She touches her mother's cheek, which is already cool. She pulls at her mother's shoulders, but the body sags in her arms.

She takes the steps again, two at a time. If she can reach the door, she can get outside to some safe place. She can almost feel the dew on the grass.

II

"So that concludes the Ghost Walk," says Annie Robinson, a tour guide, and her group applauds. "The Beverly estate used to be right here. The residence was torn down a long time ago, but that's a true story." She adds the capper: "Frances Watkins was my great-great-grandmother."

The group gasps. It's what Annie waits for, that sound, and the way their eyes go wide.

Where the Beverly mansion purportedly used to stand, there's only a depression in the ground. Across the street, there's a massive Victorian-style apartment house where Annie lives. The tree frogs in her story were inspired by the ones that live in the sycamores growing out front. She made up the garden entirely, although the ivy and the moist spots around the trees seem to evoke a lost, parklike lawn.

In any case, this is the perfect place to halt the Ghost Walk, because the Irish-themed bar where she works is a five-minute walk away. Tonight she went on a little too long, so she doesn't have time to return her oil lantern to the Chestnut Hill Welcome Center.

"So he murdered her mother," says a stylish older woman, "and probably killed all those people in the basement."

Annie's legs hurt. What a mistake to wear platform sandals to traipse around these sidewalks in the dark.

"Did she tell the police?" the woman asks. "If she didn't, then she let him get away with bumping off her own mother. Is it true?"

Annie feels her authority fading. It would be so much better if the house were still here.

"Frances died before I was born," she says, "but the story was handed down in my family. The Beverly mansion stood empty for years, and people claimed to hear screams coming from the basement."

"It's a ghost story," a man tells the stylish woman, with a wink at Frances. "It's supposed to leave you hanging."

"Well," the woman says, "she ought to know the rest of it."

"I saw leeches," a little boy announces.

"We went to a haunted house," his mother says. "He loved the leeches."

"Have you ever eaten eyeballs?" the boy asks Annie.

"No," she says. "How do they taste?"

"They're good."

"They were gumdrops," his mother says, "with M&M's stuck in."

"And there were brains," the boy says. "All squishy."

"Cold spaghetti," the mother says. "They turned off the lights and let the kids stick their hands in it."

The group is dispersing.

"There's free apple cider and cookies at the Welcome Center," Annie calls. She feels a tug of regret. She was with them for only an hour, yet their departure leaves her lonely.

She does this for fun. She loves to tell the stories of the historic old streets and old churches, and especially the tale of Frances and

Vaughan. She grew up with it. Her mother remembered seeing the Beverly mansion as a child, and taught her that Frances, who had survived and married somebody else, was her great-great-grandmother. Or something like that. Her mother's narrative kept changing.

The story makes Annie proud. Every October, for one spooky evening, she's a star.

She hurries toward Germantown Avenue, wondering if anyone guessed that pieces of her own life are embedded in the tale. An old boyfriend told her about seeing a soap woman at a museum. Her mother can be maddening and oblivious, like Frances's. Yet Annie feels she has not found the right ending. It's not enough, somehow, that Frances gets away.

The last time Annie brought up the Frances story, her mother said, "I've forgotten what's true and what isn't. I kept adding on, because you got such a kick out of it."

If it's bunk, then Annie's whole life feels like a lie.

One sandal twists, and she trips, falls, and twists her ankle. The lantern flies out of her grip and smashes on the sidewalk. Its sputters out, and the spilled kerosene smells sharp and oily.

"Are you all right?" someone asks.

It's a man from her tour, the one who winked.

"Here." He helps her to her feet.

"Thanks." She feels shaky. "These stupid shoes."

He quickly vanishes. She'd have liked to talk with him. Her hand tingles from his touch, and the brief panic of losing her balance has left a lurch in her stomach. She gathers the shards of the lantern and tosses them in a trash can. Another Ghost Walk group saunters by. She doesn't recognize the guide, a woman with silver eye shadow and a booming voice.

Annie has given the Ghost Walk for fifteen years, and overnight, it seems, she is thirty-nine. Is that old or young? She hurries along despite her aching ankle. Trees and restaurants twinkle with strands of tiny white lights. Cars rumble down the cobblestones. Every store, every bank has a glowing jack-o-lantern out front, or cornstalks and baskets of gourds. The air reeks with the raw squash odor of pumpkins and the potpourri of melting candles.

Fake cobwebs drape the doorway of the Irish bar. She lifts them and ducks inside.

It's a busy night, but Dale, the manager, seeks her out.

"Talk to me, Annie," he says. "Everywhere we go, people give my wife pigs. Knickknacks and stuff, always pigs. She doesn't even like them."

He never talks to her. It's hard to serve drinks and listen to him too. She wipes the bar with a towel.

"It started when she was little," Dale says. "She had a birthday party, and all the kids brought toy pigs. So she grows up, and we get engaged, and her friends give her a shower."

A customer signals for another beer, and Annie gets it.

"And at the shower, everything's pigs," Dale says. "There's even a clock that's a pig's face, and a curly tail going tick-tock. So we move to Philadelphia, and we don't tell a soul about the pigs. And then yesterday was her birthday, and the people at her job, they gave her a party. And guess what."

He slaps the bar, and Annie jumps.

"How far do we have to go to get away from it?" he says. His mouth opens, but it's not a laugh, it's a slack, soundless droop.

All at once, Annie is frightened. This is her life. She lives alone. There's somebody in the neighborhood who shrieks in the night for no apparent reason, as if there really is a captive in a basement, as if Frances never got out. Annie has sat up clutching the covers, her heart thrashing, her fingers slippery on the phone. *A screamer. We know about that one*, the police said when she reported it. Apartments on either side of hers have been robbed. At night, cigarette smoke wafts into her bedroom window, and gravel crunches in the alley behind the building as if someone is shifting their weight from one foot to another, hiding and watching and waiting.

"What's the matter?" Dale asks.

She shakes her head.

"Come outside," he says.

She follows him out the back door and into the humid evening. In the tiny backyard, they are surrounded by invisible revelers' laughter, chatter, and ring tones, yet they are alone, enclosed by a weathered fence. With uncanny clarity, she detects dogs' nails scraping the side-walk, and a sneeze from the direction of the old water tower.

"Tell me what's wrong," Dale says.

A bulb over the bar's rear door backlights his head. It's the first real conversation they have ever had.

"I'm scared of getting old," she says, "and there've been break-ins where I live."

"What if I gave you this bar?" Dale says. "What would you do?"

She thinks for a moment. "I'd take the Irish stew off the menu. It sucks."

"Okay. What else?"

"Keep the windows open during the day. Air it out."

"How would you manage the rowdies?" he asks.

"Same as now. Cut 'em off."

"What do you do when you're not here?" He cups her elbows in his palms and slides his hands up her arms.

"I just gave a Ghost Walk," she says. "Have you ever gone on one?"

"No."

"You're not going to give me this bar."

He plants his lips on hers and kisses her slowly, so she has time to think the word *lingering*, and all she has to do is stand there and feel how much taller he is, how big. But she tastes his worries on his lips, the dry breath of fear.

"Do you give good ghost?" he asks.

"Why do people want to be scared, when there's so much to be afraid of that's real?"

Something like anger flickers in his eyes. "That pig stuff. That's what's scary. My wife's going out of her freakin' mind."

"Get her to collect something different, to throw people off the scent."

"You think we didn't try that already?"

He jerks open the door and goes inside, and Annie follows.

Costumed celebrants stream into the bar: devil, cowboy, clown, and bride. She can't keep up with their orders. A pirate wags his tongue at her when she hands him his fried mozzarella. His teeth and earring catch the light. Such a sweet risk to take a stranger home, but she's done it before, and she'll do it again. In bed, she'll tell him about the soap woman.

Her ankle throbs, and she kicks off her shoes. The floor feels ice cold, and every passing car sends a tremor beneath her feet.

Operator

A CALL CAME IN on Christmas Eve, 1954.

"Help. My parents are hurt," the person said.

"Where are you?" I'd been a telephone operator in the Richmond, Virginia, area for two years, and I could tell when a caller was scared.

"I'm at home." The voice shook—a child's voice, a little girl's. "We live near Ashland."

A little town about half an hour away. I'd been to a Fourth of July picnic out there with Stuart Wilkinson, a man I'd hoped to marry.

"Hold on. I'll connect you with the police." I plugged in the wire, and the sheriff's office answered.

At that point, I could have hung up, but I didn't. From the child's end of the line came the faint sound of a train whistle, and I remembered the tracks that ran through Ashland's lonely pine woods. The picnic seemed long ago. I had taken cupcakes and little flags.

The deputy was trying to get the child's address. She named a main road, but no, they weren't in town.

"What's your name? and your parents'?" the deputy asked.

"Emmy Turner. Mom and Dad are . . ." she paused. "Charlie and Velma Turner. A man hurt them with a gun. Come quick."

"Is he still there?"

"No, he's gone."

"Can you give me a landmark?" he asked.

"The barn roof is red," she said, "but you can't see it in the dark."

"Who are your neighbors?" the deputy said.

"Mrs. Matthews."

The name clicked in my brain. Hazel Matthews had hosted the picnic. A strong old widow, she was a cousin of Stuart's. Lots of people were at the picnic, probably Emmy Turner and her parents among them.

"I'm on my way," the deputy said. "Can you lock the room you're in?"

"I did," she said.

I heard myself say, "Emmy, are you on the same side of the road as Mrs. Matthews?"

"Ma'am?" said the deputy, surprised I was still on the line.

"Yes," Emmy said.

The connection broke off. I yanked off my headset and laid it down. The operator beside me looked up in surprise. Our shift wasn't over.

"I have to go," I said.

✦   ✦   ✦

I had it in my genes. My grandmother was a telegraph operator for the railroad till she got glass arm. Now we'd call it carpal tunnel. One minute, you'd be tapping at your bug—that was what they called their set—and the next, your arm lay numb on the table.

I stayed single till I was thirty, then married a lineman, had three children, and wound up divorced and running a secondhand store, selling dishes and knickknacks. One day, a dog ran across wet cement outside my shop, and forty years later, the paw prints are still there, and I'm just an old lady with white hair and tennis shoes. But I'm getting way ahead of my story.

There wasn't any 9-1-1 back then, no GPS or Google. People were supposed to keep emergency numbers—fire, ambulance, and police—taped to the wall by the phone, but generally, if something bad happened, they were too rattled to do anything but call the operator. If you needed to be found, you gave directions as best you could. Houses in the country didn't have street numbers, and mail was on a rural route.

Lots of people had party lines, since they were cheaper, or no phone at all. The fastest way to get help was to go to a police station or a hospital yourself, or at least to a neighbor's house. But the 1950s were modern times. Coaxial cable was speeding up service. Two hundred and thirty thousand people lived in or near Richmond, and for every thousand, there was one operator.

When the call from the little girl came in, I was twenty-one and living with my grandmother. She was eighty-three. Her prize possession was a desk model phone with a long, coiled cord.

✦　✦　✦

MAYBE I could get Stuart to go to Ashland with me. Was my urgent mission just an excuse to see him? A few weeks earlier, he'd called and told me he was getting busier—he was a lawyer, just hired by a good firm—and wouldn't be able to see me as much. I knew what that meant. He must have met somebody else. Since then, he hadn't called.

As fast as I could, I drove from the telephone exchange building to his house in the Fan District. He had two roommates, Larry, a doctor in training—in medical residency—and Owen, who had a state job as an auditor. They'd all been friends at Hampden-Sydney and bought the house as an investment. Larry, the doctor, had a habit of saying, *Are you crazy?* He had gasflame-blue eyes and a way of lowering his head like a bull about to charge. I didn't like him. Owen was quiet, with a quick, sudden smile.

The house was all lit up, and they were having a party. Dressed-up people strolled down the sidewalk and went inside. A Christmas tree glowed through the window. I parked at the curb, and when I got out of the car, I smelled the deep blueness that meant snow was on the way. Only then did I realize I'd left my coat at work.

At the front door was Larry, the one I didn't like.

"I thought you were going to Miami," a woman sang out.

"I changed my mind," he said.

"It's eighty-five degrees down there," the woman said. "You could be driving your yummy little Corvette on the beach."

"Call me crazy." Larry lowered his head as I approached. "Well, if it isn't the operator. Hello, Janet."

"Is Stuart here? It's an emergency."

"What's the matter? Why don't you call him?" He dialed with his fingers.

"Just let me find him."

He made a show of moving aside, and I rushed past him. Inside, people were dancing and filling their plates from a big buffet. Girls flitted by in angora sweaters with tiny puffed sleeves. Something tangled around my foot, and I stumbled and fell. The music stopped.

"Easy does it," a man said—Owen, the quiet one. He helped me to my feet.

"Plug it back in," somebody yelled.

I had tripped over an extension cord. I shook it loose from my ankle. Owen let go of my hand, and there stood Stuart with his arm around a girl in a red dress.

"Merry Christmas, Janet," he said. "I'd like you to meet Winnie."

"How do you do?" the girl said, smiling. Her dress had white fur at the neck.

If we'd been in a movie, Stuart would have said, *Winnie's my sister. You thought she was my girlfriend?* and Winnie would have chimed in, *This old thing's my brother.* Stuart and I would have gotten married, with Winnie as a bridesmaid.

Instead, Larry barged in and said, "Hey, Stuart, Janet's got some kind of emergency, but she won't tell me what it is. Is this crazy or what?"

The music came back on, the Crew Cuts singing "Sh-Boom." I grabbed Stuart's hand and pulled him outside. I talked fast, and he listened with his head tilted in a way I loved and had almost forgotten about. When he heard *little girl in trouble, your cousin Hazel's neighbors,* he said all right, he'd go with me.

"Can you drive?" I said.

Yes, he would. We jumped into my car and were off. He hadn't stopped to get his coat, so both of us were cold as the dickens, plus it started to snow.

"So we're headed to a crime scene," he said. "Charlie and Velma Turner might be dead. We could get killed, too."

"That little girl is so scared. If you'd heard her voice . . ."

"Do you realize how nuts this is?"

"Now you sound like Larry." I was mad.

"It might be a hoax. It might not be the Turner child at all."

"You didn't *have* to come."

He drove fast. In a few minutes, we were out in the suburbs. Brand-new split-level houses were brilliant with decorations—floodlit Santas on rooftops, trees decked out with sapphire-blue bulbs, the most beautiful color for Christmas lights. Twenty minutes after we'd left his party, we were out in the country. The road was empty. Snow turned the ditches and fields white.

"These brakes are bad," he said. "Didn't you notice?"

"Yes, but I just haven't done anything about it." The car was my grandmother's Oldsmobile. If Winnie had something wrong with her car, I thought, he'd take care of it.

The road was so dark. I remembered fields of broom sedge shining gold as we'd left that summer picnic, and thick pine groves along the road. I could feel those woods close by, like walls. Ten more minutes passed. We didn't talk. A house loomed up. A light was on upstairs.

"Looks like Cousin Hazel's still awake," Stuart said.

He slowed and turned in at the next driveway. The headlights caught the peeling clapboards of an old farmhouse, dark inside. He pulled up and cut the engine.

"Now what?" My breath made a cloud.

Not far away, a train bowled down the tracks with its heavy sad song. Stuart and I looked at each other. His face was full of sorrow, like he could see inside the house to the hurt that had been done there. We just sat until the train whistle grew tiny, like a cat's cry.

"Where's the sheriff?" he said.

"I don't know. He said he was coming." I realized Stuart had no more idea what to do than I did. "They've heard us drive up," I said, thinking *if they're still alive.*

"All right, stay here. I'm going in."

"Be careful."

He disappeared into the darkness. After a second, I got out too. I couldn't bear the waiting, even if it was dangerous inside. Snowflakes sifted into my collar, dry as sand. The snow created enough light for me to find Stuart at a side door.

He knocked softly, then harder, and still nobody answered. He turned the knob. It wasn't locked, and we slipped inside and found ourselves in the kitchen.

It smelled of fried apples and bleach. Stuart flicked his lighter, and there was a steep, narrow staircase. We stood for a moment, listening. There was only deep silence and the churning of my heart. We moved toward the steps and climbed.

On the second floor, I threw caution to the winds and called, "Emmy?"

For a moment, nothing. Then there was the sound of a door creaking open, and running feet. My heart was jackhammering. All this was in the dark, but my eyes were adjusting. A shape took form—the little girl, Emmy.

"We've come to help you," I said. "Where are your parents?"

"Down the hall," she said in the voice I knew from the phone.

Stuart brushed past us. "Are any lights working?" he asked over his shoulder.

"No. I'll get the flashlight," Emmy said. She disappeared.

Stuart's voice reached me, muted. He was in some distant room.

"Charlie, Velma, it's me, Stuart Wilkinson. The sheriff's on the way."

"Oh God," a man's voice blared. "Help my wife. Jim Ford shot us."

" . . . get you to the hospital," Stuart was saying.

A beam of light came on: Emmy's flashlight. I followed her into a room. Stuart was bent over a bed. Emmy's light swung across a wild-faced man sitting on the floor. He wore an undershirt with odd splotches on it. After a second, I realized the spots were blood. His breathing was hard and raspy.

"My leg," he said. "He shot me in the leg."

A woman lay very still in the bed, her hair clumped on the pillow.

"Velma, hang on," Stuart said. "We're going to lift you up." He slipped his arm under her shoulders. "Janet, do you think you can grab her feet? Keep the blanket over her."

"Okay."

Emmy's beam of light trembled. The sheets looked dark, and when I touched them, they felt sticky. Velma hadn't moved or spoken. I moved my hands down her blanketed legs until I felt her ankles.

"At the count of three, lift her up," Stuart said. "Are you ready? One, two, three."

We lifted, and Velma's head fell back against Stuart's chest, her face white and slack. The salty smell of blood hit me. Velma was a big woman, and the cords in my neck strained from her weight. Stuart was taller than I was, and we moved slowly to keep our balance.

"Don't drop her," Charlie said. He crawled after us.

It took a long time for us to edge through the doorway and into the hall. Emmy shone the flashlight on a staircase, wider and shallower than the kitchen steps.

Charlie limped and hopped, clinging to the banister.

"I owe him money," he said. "I got Emmy to write down his name, so if Velma and me didn't make it . . ."

"How come the electricity's off?" Stuart said.

"I got behind on the bills," said Charlie, "but the phone's still on. Emmy called for help."

"It was me," I said. "She got me."

"Easy does it," Stuart said. "One more step to go."

We reached the first floor. Emmy flung open the front door, and the night air breezed into the already cold hallway.

"Set her down, Janet," Stuart said. "I'll get the car."

We lowered Velma to the floor. Charlie and Emmy and I waited with her. Still she didn't move or speak. Charlie bent his face down to hers.

"Velma, honey," he kept saying.

My Oldsmobile came bumping across the yard. The snow had stopped. Beneath bare trees, the ground glistened. Velma didn't make a sound as Stuart and I loaded her into the back. Charlie crawled into the passenger seat up front, turned around, and stroked Velma's cheek.

"I'll take you to Cousin Hazel's," Stuart said. "We can't wait for the police."

Emmy and I crouched on the floor of the Oldsmobile, my face level with Velma's head. Emmy found her mother's hand under the blanket and clutched it. The smell of blood filled the car. The tires spun in the powdery snow until it bucked free.

The motion of the car felt rough and powerful. Squatting on the floor, I couldn't move. In a few minutes, we stopped, and I understood we'd reached Mrs. Matthews's house. Stuart ran up to the porch. I got out of the car and held out my hand to Emmy.

"Go with the lady," Charlie said. "I'll look after your mother."

Emmy's hand was ice cold, but she let me lead her to the house.

"Cousin Hazel!" Stuart was thumping the brass knocker.

The porch light came on, the door swept open, and there was Hazel Matthews in an old-fashioned nightcap, her face wide and honest, like I remembered.

"Stuart, what on earth?" she said.

"Charlie and Velma Turner have been hurt. I'm taking them to the hospital. Can their daughter stay with you?"

"Of course," Hazel said, and he was gone. The car door slammed, and the Oldsmobile rolled down the driveway and turned onto the road. Hazel looked at me. Behind bifocals, her eyes were mystified, but clear and lively.

"Come in and get warm, both of you." She brought Emmy and me inside. "It's Janet, right?"

"Yes. Janet Morton."

She got us settled on a sofa under a knitted afghan. I hugged Emmy close. She didn't say anything and didn't cry.

"Are you hurt?" I asked. "Did he do anything to you?"

"No. I hid in my room. He didn't see me."

Hazel went into the kitchen. There was a rattle of pots and pans. In a few minutes, she came out with a tray of cinnamon toast, hot cocoa for Emmy, and coffee for me.

"I'll call the sheriff and tell him you-all are here," she said. When I reached for the coffee cup, she said, "Would you like to wash up?"

My hands were bloody, was what she meant. In her bathroom, I turned on the hot water and worked the soap to lather. There were stains on my dress, and my face in the mirror was chalky and shocked.

Next I got Emmy, took her to the sink, and washed her mother's blood from her hands.

Back in the living room, we sat down, and Hazel said, "Janet, how about . . . ?"

She held out a bottle of brandy. I lifted my cup, and she spiked it. I took a big gulp and felt grateful.

"You gave me a flag," Emmy said to me. "I still have it." She sipped the hot cocoa. She was pretty the way a thin little cat would be pretty.

"Do you think you can you tell us what happened?" I asked.

She didn't answer for a long time. Hazel and I waited.

"The man fussed at Dad," Emmy said. "He wouldn't go away. He came upstairs and acted like they had money somewhere. He kept yelling. Then I heard *bam, bam, bam*." Her voice trailed off. "Will Mom be all right?"

"She's safe. She'll get the best care."

Emmy's face crumpled. Hazel held her and rocked her back and forth. She had heard her parents get shot. I could hardly take that in.

"There, there," Hazel said. She wiped Emmy's tears with her fingers. "You're very tired. How about if I tuck you in? I'll check on you a little later." She took Emmy upstairs.

When she came back, she said, "I found her an old teddy bear, and she went right to sleep. You should, too. This house has plenty of room."

"I don't think I could sleep."

Hazel sat down beside me and bunched the afghan in her hands.

"This is the worst thing that's ever happened here," she said. "There's never been this kind of," and she paused, "violence."

Velma's head falling back—I couldn't bear to think about her.

"How old is Emmy?" I asked.

"She's six." Hazel's forehead puckered. "How did you know they needed help? Why did you and Stuart go over there?"

I told her everything.

"Think of the odds," she said, "that you were the one to get that call." We sat there with our separate thoughts. She went upstairs, came back, and said, "Sound asleep."

"That's a mercy."

"She can stay with me as long as she needs to."

A mantel clock ticked.

"Do you think you could manage some fruitcake?" Hazel asked.

It was homemade and delicious, with candied cherries. I ate two slices. Somebody knocked on the door—the sheriff. He'd been to the hospital and talked with Charlie Turner and Stuart. A deputy had tracked down and arrested the man who had attacked the Turners. I talked with the sheriff, called my grandmother, and fell asleep on the sofa.

✦ ✦ ✦

IN Miami, people were driving convertibles with the tops down, guzzling fancy drinks from coconut halves, and playing in the surf. Nowhere else was the sky so blue or so beautiful. Stuart's roommate Larry described all this as he drove me home the next day. He'd been to Miami the previous winter.

"You'd love it," he said. "You should see it sometime. It's crazy."

The Turners were improving. Stuart had called me at Hazel's with the news. The bullet in Charlie's leg had missed the bone. He was already up and walking, but Velma's situation was far more delicate. One of her lungs had collapsed. *She's still critical,* Stuart had said, *but she's awake, and they're saying she'll pull through. Your car's here at the house, but I'm beat, Janet. I was at the hospital all night. Larry offered to pick you up and take you home. Is that okay?*

Of course, I'd said. *Get some rest.* Yet it hurt that he wasn't coming for me himself. How stupid that was, to even think that way.

Hazel had fixed a big breakfast. Emmy understood her parents were better, and she was hungry for the ham, eggs, and waffles. I ate too, and took a bath, and Hazel loaned me clean clothes. By the time Larry showed up, it was almost noon, on a cloudy, silvery day.

So I got in the Corvette, and Larry and I sped along. The road was clear, but snow clung to the ditch banks. In the low-slung car, I felt off-balance, my nerves jangled. Woods and fields raced by.

"Would you please not drive so fast?" I said.

He slowed down, but barely.

"Velma Turner's got a long recovery ahead," he said. "Traumatic pneumothorax—that's a collapsed lung. Heavy blood loss . . ."

Suddenly I couldn't stand it, couldn't stand *him*.

"Don't say anything," I said. "Don't say one single thing. Just take me home."

He slowed down a little more. "You don't like me, do you, Janet?"

"No, I don't. And I'll probably get fired."

He pulled the car to the side of the road and laughed so hard he had to rest his head on the steering wheel. "Do you always cause so much excitement? The party wasn't nearly as fun after you left."

"I didn't know what else to do."

"I don't think you'll lose your job," he said. "Don't worry about it."

A cardinal swooped by, brilliant against the snow. The car's engine ticked, and all around, the countryside was quiet. I remembered it was Christmas. Christmas Day, 1954.

"You ought to get a medal," he said. "I mean it. You and Stuart saved those people."

"That little girl needs some presents."

"The stores are all closed. Otherwise, I'd drive you downtown, and you could go shopping. I don't have to be at work till five o'clock."

Had I heard right? "Well, that's nice of you."

"I can be nice," he said. "I started to drive your car out here, but not with those brakes. Want me to get them fixed?"

Again, had I heard right?

"Sure. Thank you," but I couldn't think about the car. I was thinking about Emmy and Hazel. We would be friends, I hoped, and in the years to come, we could—and we did—talk about that terrible night.

Larry reached over and tucked my hair behind my ear. "If the gunshots didn't kill those people, your brakes could have."

I just looked at him.

"If anything happened to you, I'd be very upset," he said.

"You would?"

"I've always liked you, Janet, even though you think I'm a rat." He laughed.

And I cried. The tears came in a storm. I cried and cried, blew my nose, let out a big breath, and felt better.

"I like you a whole lot," Larry said. He wasn't laughing anymore.

I looked into those gasflame eyes.

That quick, I was in a new life. I saw the future: we would fall in love, break up, and get back together a million times. It might even work out. I let a moment go by, and then I leaned toward him. He put his arms around me and kissed me.

It was crazy, it was nuts. I kissed him back.

Hay Season

I

DORIS Wilson, the home health aide who cared for Mr. Carter on night shift, kept track of how long he hadn't slept. How could anybody, let alone an eighty-seven-year-old, survive nine such nights? Silent and agitated, he steered his walker from sofa to armchair while Doris tried to keep him from falling.

At dawn, she greeted the next aide, a new girl named Heather.

"He was awake all night," Doris said. "This is the tenth day."

"What does his doctor say?" Heather asked.

"They don't know what to do about it." Doris packed up her pillow, afghan, and sudoku book. Not much chance to use them lately. She showed Heather where everything was—medications, logbook, and his clothing and supplies.

"Mr. Carter," she said, "I'll see you tonight."

A few months ago, he could still talk. He didn't anymore, although he could hear. Doris patted his arm.

"I've never seen such a big house," Heather said, glancing up at the high ceiling of the living room, which had been converted into a bedroom for Mr. Carter.

"You'll be too busy to look around," Doris said.

"Heading home to sleep?"

"First I've got to milk the cows." Doris and her husband Floyd raised dairy cows. Money was too tight to hire anybody.

"Do you milk them by hand?" Heather asked.

"You hook 'em up to machines. I'd rather milk cows than deal with Meemaw. My mother-in-law lives with us. Ninety-eight, a real monster."

Doris caught herself. She didn't want Heather to go sour on her, like other aides had done, two in particular, Donald and Vicky. She'd made the mistake of complaining to them about Meemaw, and they'd egged her on, pretending sympathy, then turned on her for reasons unknown, and got her in trouble with the manager, saying she didn't keep a close enough eye on Mr. Carter, when they were the ones taking smoke breaks. The porch was littered with butts. When one was on duty, the other came by and visited: they let that be known, showing off how close they were.

Mr. Carter gripped his walker and struggled to his feet, and Doris ditched her bags and rushed to him.

"Heather, when he's on the move, stay close."

Heather looked baffled, and Doris felt exasperated. She steadied Mr. Carter as he tottered to a window and stared out at his neglected fields. By now, September, all the hay in Virginia should have been cut twice. Mr. Carter's land hadn't been mowed in forever, but there was no one to care for the farm, the pastures were empty, and his children had moved away.

In the distance, a rooster called, *cock-a-doodle-do.* Heather held nicotine-stained fingers to her mouth. She had tattooed knuckles and a bruised arm.

"Chickens?" she said.

"You're out in the country, girl," Doris said.

She could see all the way through Heather's life: a dark, smelly apartment in town, a mean man storming in and out, Heather choosing a polyester smock from the rack in the Best Care office and dozing through the Certified Nursing Assistant course.

Doris guided Mr. Carter back to an armchair. His china-blue eyes gazed into hers. He must be so tired.

"Listen up, Heather," she said. "You've got eight hours. Then Vicky or Donald'll be here for third shift, and you're done, but in the meantime, call me if you need to." She wrote down her number. Heather looked at it blankly and put it in her pocket.

Out in the driveway, Doris inhaled the cool, beautiful morning. She craned her neck at the house. She doubted she would ever see all those rooms unless he died and his children held the gathering there. Other clients had died, and she had gone to their funerals, but the thought of losing Mr. Carter hurt her heart.

She could ask Floyd to come over and bush-hog the overgrown fields, but he would say he was too busy, and Meemaw would back him up, and Doris would wish she'd never mentioned it.

Driving home, she vowed to avoid Meemaw for the rest of the day. After milking, she would head to the pantry, where she had created a cozy nest for herself. Beneath shelves that held canned squash, tomatoes, beans, pickles, and jugs of Floyd's hard cider, there was a sleeping bag that belonged to her grandson Ryan. He was far away in New Orleans, Teaching for America, but the sleeping bag held his puppyish scent, and it was her refuge.

Why, there she was in the pantry, toeing off her sneakers and sliding into the bulky bag. Had she already tended to the cows? Yes, there was clay on her shoes. Floyd was out at the barn feeding the dogs. She'd told him about Mr. Carter's fields, and he said he couldn't do a thing about it. She snapped back, *Well, I work all night, plus I take care of your mother. I don't ask you for much.*

"Doris, are you here?" Meemaw's wheelchair squeaked on the kitchen linoleum. "I see your purse. Where are you?"

"Hiding from you," Doris whispered.

"Let's see what's in here," Meemaw crooned. "Sue-doh-koo?"

Doris clenched her fists. Finally the chair creaked away, and she stretched into the bag, praying Mr. Carter would sleep. Her mind roamed the unknown reaches of his house. She had never been beyond the front rooms and the kitchen, but Donald and Vicky had bragged about finding a ballroom with a marble mantelpiece. *He doesn't even know whether you're there or not,* they said. Doris would love to see those places, but it was wrong to leave him alone and wrong to go roving around without permission. She had hinted to the manager to pop in on that third shift, but it wouldn't happen. Vicky and Donald were Teflon.

How was it she was sixty-five all of a sudden? She remembered childhood—her drunk father's fist against her jaw, her mother saying, *Don't make him mad.* There was church. She still went, but it was Baptists with their angry God.

She had Ryan, even if he was far away, and Mr. Carter, needing her. She dozed off imagining the rooms she had never seen.

II

Ryan Wilson had fallen in love, but not with Sarah, his fiancée, who was beautiful and perfect. No, he was in love with Brittni, a living fantasy in Honors English, whose silent laugh made her body ripple. This morning, he asked her when her birthday was, and he spent lunch period figuring out how many days until she turned eighteen, at which point he planned to marry her, except by then he'd be married to Sarah.

He held up *Dr. Jekyll and Mr. Hyde* and asked the class, "What's at stake in this story?"

Brittni's lips moved, but she spoke so softly he couldn't hear her.

"Why don't you kiss her, Ryan?" bawled a bumpy-faced girl named Kayla.

The bell rang, and students flung themselves out the door. Kayla departed with a leer, but Brittni stayed, leaning against Ryan's desk. How lovely her eyes were, green, flecked with black.

"I couldn't hear what you said," he said.

"About the book, you mean?" Cinnamon breath.

"If you don't tell me, I'll wonder for the rest of my life."

She rippled. "I don't remember."

"A woman like you, Brittni, you'll change the world."

"You think?" She gave a shy, gorgeous grin.

"I'll write you a great recommendation," he said, "for college."

"I don't want to go to college." She tapped a yellow highlighter against her cheek.

His next class was assembling, students trickling in.

"What *do* you want?" he asked.

She checked her phone.

"There's mustard on your tummy." She glided away.

He looked down at his shirt. There was only a dot, but because she noticed, he'd wash it out. He galloped to the restroom. At grimy sinks, boys stubbed out cigarettes and retreated. He was proud to see how scared of him they were, yet when they were gone, his solitude felt strange and perilous.

"Rye-un!" came a taunt from the hallway.

He jerked the door, but it was jammed. How stupid he was. Third time he'd been tricked like this. He took out his phone to call the principal. No, Mr. Jones was already disgusted with him. He'd have to get out on his own. He stepped on a toilet, climbed to the top of a stall, and balanced one foot on a high windowsill.

His leg trembled. To get out of the building, he'd have to break glass and jump a long way to the ground. While he wobbled, a horrible realization dawned. When Brittni looked at her phone and said, *There's mustard on your tummy,* she must have been giving or receiving a message. She set him up. Had she somehow put the mustard there, or dabbed her highlighter on his shirt?

"Kinda dangerous, don't you think?" somebody said—it was Kayla, popping out from the next stall, where evidently she had been hiding.

She gazed up at him, her foreshortened face impish and ugly. His keys slid out of his pocket and plunked into the toilet.

"Whoa, Ryan. No need to throw things."

Awkwardly he gripped the top of the stall, worked his way down, and landed in a heap. Kayla brayed with laughter.

"Go fishing, Ryan."

Gritting his teeth, he stuck his hand in the toilet and retrieved his keys.

"Need to pee, handsome?" she said. "I can wait."

He didn't need to when he came in, but now he did, and of course he wouldn't, with her there. Rinsing his keys, he had never been angrier.

"I'll get you kicked out of school for this, Kayla."

"Okay with me."

"I'm not going to stand here and argue with you."

"But you are." She chortled. "Look, Ryan, I already have a boy-friend. He says *fang-ger* for finger and sits around in his underwear."

"So?"

"I deserve better. Maybe you don't want me now, but someday you'll want me bad."

"I want nothing to do with you."

"The first day, you told us you're getting married. Does Sarah know about Brittni?"

"There's nothing to know." Chilling—their names in her mouth.

Her crooked teeth flashed. "Wanna get out of here, cupcake?"

"Yes, damn it."

"There's a password. They won't open the door till you say it."

He couldn't help but ask, "Is Brittni out there?"

"Sure. Everybody is. She's preggers, did you know?"

He gasped. Triumphantly, Kayla nodded.

"You're lying," he said. "Whose is it?"

"Ask her."

Out in the hallway, the din rose, a sickening chant: "Rye-un! Rye-un and Kay-lahhh!"

His mouth was completely dry.

"All right," he said, "what's the password?"

"Teach for America."

He barked it. The door swung open, and he fled through the mob.

✦   ✦   ✦

"SOCK feet, Ryan," Sarah said when he burst into their apartment. "I just washed the floor."

He bent over, ripped off his shoes, and raced to the bathroom.

"Did you get the muffalettas?" Sarah called.

They had a rule: no talking when one of them was in the bath-room. He didn't answer, which was breaking another rule, because they *were* allowed to talk in emergencies. The relief of peeing was the only thing holding off the moment when he would have to admit he forgot the muffalettas, even though Sarah had texted three times to remind him. She could have picked them up, since she was home all day. He wasn't supposed to say *just planning the wedding.* She was also looking for a job.

He zipped and flushed.

Could there have been some plausible agenda on Brittni's part other than humiliating him? *There's mustard on your tummy.* Was it possible she was crushing on him? *Tummy* was intimate, sexy even. Maybe she asked Kayla for help. Maybe Brittni was supposed to be the one in the boys' room, waiting for him, but Kayla muscled in and messed up the plan.

There, he'd figured it out. Brittni was probably crying her pretty eyes out. He'd forgive her, not that her little prank was okay. *Watch out, Beautiful, it's your turn next.* Were all the girls in love with him? Kayla, propositioning him. *Someday you'll want me bad.* Sex with her would be mature and wolfish, and yes, part of him wanted it, but not like he wanted Brittni.

Preggers cut through him.

He took off his shirt and scrubbed the yellow dot to no avail. Sarah would make him apply stain remover. He hurled the shirt to the floor. Brittni was the only girl he'd ever love. She could have her baby no matter whose it was, and he'd adopt it.

The first time he was trapped in the boys' restroom, he'd told Sarah about it, but not the second time, because by then he was in love with Brittni and everything about school was secret. Yet he sensed Sarah suspected something. Last night, she got hold of his gradebook, read through the roster, and zeroed in: *Brittni sounds like a stripper's name.* She'd launched into a merry monologue, which led to her favorite names for the children they would presumably create together, and it was too late to stop all this, because the save-the-date magnets were in the mail.

So he couldn't tell her anything about today unless he told everything, which maybe he could do if something crazy happened when he opened the door, like she gave the ring back and said, *We're through, get out,* or better yet, she was the one moving out. He'd been hoping she'd fall in love with the fat guy next door, who also seemed to be home with nothing to do. She could have the sofa, which they bought together, and he couldn't wait to be rid of that antique she cooed about, her *little fruitwood chest*. The word *fruitwood* annoyed the hell out of him.

But she had mailed the save-the-date magnets. She had narrowed the styles of magnets to three and made him pick. That's how she liked for them to make decisions. God, he was sick of it. He hated his picture on the magnets, like a little boy. He needed to grow a mustache or a beard, and work out and get bigger.

He yanked open the door. Sarah was right there, wearing her *I want an explanation* face, but before he could open his mouth, his phone rang. It was his grandmother, a thousand miles away. He'd never been so glad to talk to her.

"I had a bad dream, Ryan," she said. "The kids set the school on fire, and you were stuck inside."

"I'm fine, Grandma. Did you get the magnet?" He made himself smile at Sarah.

"What magnet?" Grandma said. "Guess where I am, honey."

He concentrated until a picture came to him—the canned food and crooked shelves of his childhood. "The pantry?"

"You are so smart," Grandma said.

✦ ✦ ✦

Three days ago, Sarah had entered the post office and joined a slow-moving line. She clutched the box of magnets to her stomach and wondered, Is this how it feels to be pregnant?

"There's stuff they won't ship," said a man behind her.

She turned around to find a puckish face. "Like what?"

"A tarantula," he said. "I tried to mail one to my ex-wife."

Sarah laughed and couldn't stop. Other people in line guffawed and cackled. Pleasure swept through Sarah's whole body, as if she'd dived into a pool. People wouldn't have laughed so long in Pittsburgh, her hometown, where she and Ryan would be married. *She* wouldn't have laughed so hard in Pittsburgh, yet here among strangers, she could enjoy herself.

It was her turn at the counter. She paid for a hundred "Love" stamps and set about sticking them on the envelopes, which she'd addressed in calligraphy. At *Floyd and Doris Wilson*, Ryan's grandparents, she paused.

She'd met them when she and Ryan graduated from college. Excited about moving to New Orleans, showing off her engagement ring, she'd known what she wanted.

Well, things had changed.

The laughter was the signal she needed. She picked up a trash can and swept all the stamps and envelopes into it. There went *Floyd and Doris Wilson*. The weatherbeaten old couple had seemed nice enough, but now she would never have to worry about what they might say or think or do.

Later, back home, she re-enacted the sweeping gesture in front of the bedroom mirror. It looked like a dance move. Yet by the time Ryan got home, she'd slipped back into routine, with fabric samples laid out so he could choose the tablecloths for the reception.

For two days, she went around in a fog, until last night, soliloquizing about baby names, she was struck by the realization that she didn't want kids for a long time and maybe never. The thought of breaking the engagement filled her with exhilaration. Ryan would ask, *Is there some other guy?* Oh, there would be, and she could hardly wait. Somewhere in New Orleans, a rugged stranger was surely yearning to meet her.

But she was afraid to tell Ryan the truth. Had she decided, or not? She was stuck with him in their living room, and he was on the phone with his grandmother, asking, "Did you get the magnet?"

By now, the magnets were on a garbage scow headed to China, unless somebody had dug them out of the trash can. Sarah pictured a hippie chick sticking them on a fridge. The girl's friends would ask, *Who the hell are Ryan and Sarah?* and she would tilt a beer to her lips and say, *I have no idea,* and everyone would laugh. Sarah wanted to be that carefree girl and not the coiffed, matronly person on the magnets.

III

At suppertime, Doris found Heather, not Donald or Vicky, feeding Mr. Carter a hamburger patty, creamed corn, and peas.

"You worked a double shift?" Doris asked. "What happened?"

"Nobody showed up," Heather said. "I called the office, and they said Vicky and Donald both quit." She patted Mr. Carter's lips with a napkin and told him, "You did good."

"You could have called me," Doris said. "I could've come early." *Vicky and Donald quit.* Her heart sang.

"I knew you were tired," Heather said. "Look, I made him a banana pudding."

From outside, in the dusk, came a mechanical growl. Heather's head whipped around.

"A tractor," Doris said, feeling as surprised as Heather looked.

They peered out the kitchen window. Yes, it was Floyd's.

"I asked my husband to cut the hay, but I didn't think he was going to."

"But it'll be dark soon," said Heather.

The headlights came on.

"Wow," Heather said.

"Look, Mr. Carter," Doris said, "your hay's getting cut. My husband's doing it."

He actually smiled *thank you* right into her eyes, and just like that, the agitation went out of him, and he was easy again, like the not-sleeping was a coat he took off.

Heather gathered her things and said goodnight. Doris spooned banana pudding into a dish and fed Mr. Carter. When he didn't open his mouth anymore, she knew he had had enough.

"Are you ready for bed?" she asked, and he nodded.

She accomplished his bath, dressed him in clean pajamas, and brushed his teeth. She fluffed the pillow, helped him into bed, and took a seat on a chair beside him.

Light from Floyd's tractor shone through the windows and crossed the dark walls in watery waves. Mr. Carter followed it with his eyes. Was he picturing how his fields would look with the hay cut and drying out for baling? You could see a long way across mowed land. Did he remember the Blue Ridge Mountains in the distance, the same as when he was a boy?

She knew she should be grateful he was calm and Floyd was being nice. Heather too. That was a lot, yet her heart was aching as it had ached all her life.

It was Ryan. He was in trouble, she knew it. There'd been something in his voice today. He was too young to get married, and he was as weak and innocent as a kitten, with his head of bobbing curls. Was he in love with some little teenage girl? She imagined students throwing their desks across the room while he flapped his arms and shouted.

Swift as deer, stripes of light chased across Mr. Carter's blanketed form.

"Who are you?" he asked.

His voice was the way she remembered, courtly and old-fashioned. After his long silence, she was startled.

"I'm Doris. Doris Wilson from Best Care."

"Would you like to see my house?"

"I'd love to."

She held her breath, but he didn't say anything more. Those might be the last words he ever spoke, and he had said them to her.

The sound of mowing faded. Floyd must be almost to the woods.

She rose from the chair. Not long ago, Mr. Carter would have played the role of genial host, leading a visitor on a guided tour, but never again. With his blessing, she would explore on her own. At last she would see what Vicky and Donald had talked about—the long hallways, the bedrooms one after another, a ballroom where people must have danced long ago.

"Thank you, Mr. Carter," she said. "I'll look around a little bit, and I'll be back soon."

She had wanted this, yet she was afraid. It would mean bumping into walls, finding her way through doors where there might be anything on the other side, and staircases where she could slip and fall. And it would mean leaving him alone.

"I won't be long," but she hovered, her hand on the back of the chair. What was she waiting for? Everybody would say how silly she was to hesitate, how stupid. *He invited you. You, of all people. Go on.*

Mr. Carter's eyes were closed, and his breath made a sigh. *Wish, wish.* He was asleep. She sat down and stayed.

A Thousand Stings

for Julie and Hilary

my sisters

I

Glen Allen, Virginia
May 1967

Girls are chasing Raymond West, fifth- and sixth-grade girls in a posse that formed spontaneously, like a tornado. School's out for the day, the air sweet and heady from spirea bushes blooming by the door. Buses are lined up, but nobody's boarding, because girls are chasing Raymond West, the handsomest boy in school, never mind he's only ten years old. He's fast, so fast he's expected to win the fifty-yard dash when Field Day rolls around. He goes by Ray now: Ray West. It's a grown-up nickname, a fact not lost on his admirers. Already there's something manly about him.

The older girls are dressed in party clothes, because this was Chorus Day. Squealing, they feel beautiful. Their ruffles and puffy skirts put wind in their feet.

The Chorus Day songs still ring in eight-year-old Shirley Lloyd's ears as she, a third grader, hangs back to watch the chase. Her favorites are "Edelweiss," the soaring "Shenandoah," and the tuneful "Inchworm," and there's a song about wandering that makes her eyes fill with tears of emotion. Her older sister Patty, one of Ray West's pursuers, is one of the best singers in the sixth grade, with a low, sweet alto. Their mother has taught them that voices in the lower register are best: *Sopranos have such unfortunate speaking voices.*

Another one of the choral stars, Patty's friend Evie Cartwright, steps back from chasing Ray, catches her breath, and, as if reading Shirley's mind, launches into a solo, shading her eyes to watch the hunt continue without her:

> *I love to go a-wandering, beneath the clear blue sky,*
> *I love to go a-wandering, beneath the clear blue sky.*
> *Valderee, valderahh! Be-neath the . . . clear . . . blue . . . sky.*

The song is exquisite, no matter that *valderee* and *valderahh* are mystery words. Shirley wants Evie to sing it again, but she's afraid to ask her: Evie is three years older. Stumbling, running harder as he realizes the girls aren't giving up, Ray drops his lunch box, a blue metal one with an astronaut on the front. Girls' shoes clunk against it and knock it toward Shirley. She picks it up, unable to believe her luck, never mind the fresh dent in the astronaut's face, right in his smile. She rubs the dent, but it stays.

Astronaut lunch boxes aren't as popular as they used to be. Since January, when those three astronauts died in a fire on their launching pad, fewer boys want to explore outer space. Shirley has heard the names so often, she has them memorized: Gus Grissom, Roger Chaffee, and Edward White.

Ray sprints ahead.

"Man, he's fast," a boy near Shirley murmurs, bowled over, in a voice so full of reverence that it is utterly flat, grave, the tone of a TV announcer narrating a rocket launch.

Tucking the lunch box under her arm, Shirley chugs alongside the pack of older girls. Her sister Patty pulls ahead of the others and harries Ray into a corner of the chain-link fence, where he buckles to his knees. Pushing out her chin, lowering her face to his, Patty makes kissing noises, exaggerated for comedy. Ray flushes scarlet all the way to his scalp. Shirley wonders how his face would feel in her hands and realizes that other girls too will dream about his bristly hair and warm, bullet-shaped head.

Giving up, Ray waves his arms to ward off the girls, but isn't that a smile making his cheeks bulge? Oh, they got him, but he won. His grin shows it. He could have any one of them as his girlfriend, even the older ones. He could have anybody he wants, and that will be true all of his good-looking life, and the girls know it too. Screeching, triumphant, they join hands in a tight circle around him and dance until their skirts ride over their white tights and their patent-leather shoes skid out from under them.

Patty's in love with him. Shirley can't tease Patty about this. It matters too much. Shirley is surrounded by secrets, close enough to touch. Patty keeps a locked diary, and so do her friends. They take the diaries to school and brandish them, making sure it is known that much of importance is recorded there. The golden keys are tiny. Bobby Scott got hold of Evie Cartwright's key and twisted it between his fingers until it snapped in two, while Evie screamed and whacked at him with a diary covered in quilted pink plastic and thick as a Bible.

Ray's astronaut lunch box is more marvelous than any diary, and it's right here in Shirley's hands. Ray doesn't know she has it. She can try to get the dent out and then give it back to him, earning his gratitude. Ray West officially replaces Prince Valiant, of the comic strip, as her idol. Fingering the metal fasteners on the lunch box, she allows Princess Aleta to reclaim Prince Valiant. *You can have him back.*

The girls' commotion makes a cicada-like din, echoing off the brick walls of the school's two stories and bell tower. As the group breaks apart, Ray bolts for his bus, and Shirley reaches a conclusion to a problem that has bothered her for a long time, something that has nothing to do with the scene in front of her.

She is tired of being late to school. Every morning, her sisters dillydally, Patty a worse offender than six-year-old Diana. By the time the three of them reach the end of their driveway, the bus has usually come and gone. When Shirley complains, their mother defends the sisters and refuses to let Shirley walk down the driveway by herself. All three must stick together. Their father agrees with Shirley, but he won't contradict her mother. When the girls miss the bus, their mother or father must drive them, an activity that somehow causes further lateness.

All of Shirley's teachers have been baffled that she is so often tardy, when she is otherwise a good student. She hates the very word *tardy*. Only teachers use it.

From now on, she decides, she will walk to school. Her resolution thrills her. She gets up early anyway, at 6:30, when it's still cold. Gets up, gets dressed, puts coffee and water in the percolator, and plugs it in as her mother has taught her to do, then makes the rounds to wake up the family. Her father rises, but her mother and sisters stay in their beds, lumps beneath the covers, no matter how she hectors them. She turns on her heel and leaves their rooms in turn: her parents', Patty's, and Diana's. Next, she feeds the family's many cats, pouring dry food into saucers on the porch. The number of cats changes according to birth rates. Right now, there are ten: four tabbies, two solid black, one gray, one orange, and two black and white. After tending them, she plays solitaire, five, six, seven games. She imagines "Solitaire" as a dragon, an enemy, but you have to respect him, because he's smart. Her father comes down to the kitchen, smiles at the card games, and pours grape-flavored Hi-C for her and for himself. The very idea of school makes her too nervous to eat breakfast. She hopes her father won't fix eggs. He burns them.

Her mother keeps track of everything. Her father doesn't. During the winter, her mother was in the hospital with pneumonia, and her father forgot to make her bathe. Now and then he reminded her sisters, but Shirley was overlooked, to her joy. Three weeks and no bath, and nobody the wiser. So cold in winter, that bathroom with linoleum tiles coming unglued from the floor and the tub taking so long to fill, the well water so hard with minerals that bubbles won't form no matter what kind of soap you use. The very first night her mother was home, she made Shirley take a bath. She sat on top of the closed toilet, supervising Shirley and Diana, who were small enough to fit in the tub together. To Shirley, the water felt unfamiliar, as if she were a cat stepping into a stream. Her mother looked so tired, hunched in her soft pink robe with a smell of medicine clinging to her. She kept saying, *It's good to be home.*

Now her mother is recovered, and winter is far away, like a witch packed into a closet between bales of straw, dozing, eyes dreamy, threats gone.

Despite the cold bathroom, Shirley loves their big old house. She doesn't mind its drafts, its creaking floors, and the radiators' habit of emitting a single, stealthy dark syllable like an intruder's footstep. She loves the high ceilings, big rooms, and long hallways. It's an old farmhouse, her parents say. The big barn and the fields once provided a livelihood, back at the turn of the century, when Glen Allen was known for its dairy production. Sometimes Shirley's father, who grew up on a farm, talks about wanting to get a few cows, but her mother demurs, and the barn, with its stalls, stanchions, and friendly, musty odor, stays vacant except for mice.

Who lived here before us? Shirley has asked, and her mother answered, *A family named Manning. They were nice. The day we moved in, you were only a few months old. Mrs. Manning was putting the last few things in their truck, and she told me she'd been up and down the stairs so many times, she didn't think she could ever climb steps again.* Ever since then, whenever Shirley finds herself going up and down the stairs a lot, she thinks of Mrs. Manning and feels a sense of kinship.

Shirley's mind runs over all of this and back again to now. Ray West's lunch box in her hands makes her feel something new is beginning.

This is Friday, so tomorrow morning she can sleep late. The realization floods her with relief. It's Friday, and her mother will fix stuffed peppers for supper. The bright green peppers were on the kitchen counter this morning. Soon she'll be home with the cats. Their habits delight her—the stropping of claws on a big elm root, like crazed harpists plucking invisible strings; the wild exuberance of kittens at play. Their conflicts break her heart—their murderous fights, their hunger. When Leopold, the old tomcat, gnaws ravenously on one scrap of gristly meat and plants his foot on another, growling to keep the others away, she understands when you're that hungry, sharing is just too hard.

In small herds, children move toward the yellow buses. A big boy yells out a stale joke: "Gimme a new fanny! This one's cracked!"

Patty sticks her nose in the air, registering disgust. She would deny she ever chased anybody, let alone a boy. Patty's getting flighty. Just last night, she pitched a fit because their mother refused to let her change her name to "Melissa." She ran to her room and cried extra loud, so the family would realize she had been deeply wronged. "Michelle" was her second choice, and after that, probably "Hayley," she confided to Shirley between sobs, but their mother wouldn't hear of it.

Patty veers away from Shirley to find her friends. Patty better hurry. The buses are about to leave. Ray's goes first, pulling out of the circular drive, bearing him away. Shirley climbs on her bus and sits by the window, planning. She'll ride the bus in the afternoons, but not the mornings. She will have to leave early to walk to school, and if her parents try to stop her, well, she won't let them.

While children file past her, finding seats, she covers the distance in her mind. Her house is the first stop in the afternoons, the last in the mornings. The distance from the house to the end of the driveway, where the road begins, is far, and it's so much farther to school—quick in a car or on the bus, but farther than she has ever walked. Her perception of time and space will be forever shaped by that configuration. Where the driveway meets the road: that's the edge of the world, amazing as the ocean.

Mountain Road is narrow and flat, the mountains hours away.

Shirley and her sisters sometimes play a dangerous game their parents don't know about. *I dare you. Step into the road.* One at a time they do this, but linger only an instant. Luckily there is little traffic. If a car ever came around the bend, Shirley would rush out and save Patty and Diana, lift them up and carry them into the sky. She would save them from anything, including the vandals who sometimes blow up mailboxes along Mountain Road. Her parents talk about them as if they're a family: the Vandals. In case the Vandals or any such criminals come to the house, the Lloyds have an escape plan: scatter, run to the woods, and hide until Daddy finds you, or Mama, Shirley's mother says, speaking of herself in third person as she does in times of seriousness. *Wait for Mama to come.*

Shirley has practiced gathering cats in her arms, to save them too if the Vandals come. Silently, she races after them, grabbing scruffs and tails. Once she got hold of four at the same time, staggering under their writhing weight until they exploded from her arms. Two she can manage, or maybe one full-grown and a box of kittens, can clutch them all the way to the woods. The old tomcat, Leopold, worries her. He's quick to scratch a grasping hand. He would have to escape on his own. He would be all right, she tries to assure herself. He'd find a hiding place.

So she'll walk to school. She will step out into the road and keep on going, like an explorer. Explorers are her favorite subject. What glorious names they have—Hernando de Soto, Ponce de Leon, Balboa, Magellan. When she reported to her mother that Vasco da Gama probably beat Columbus to the New World, her mother looked vexed.

Vasco da Gama? she said, as if the name were a bad word. *I've never heard of him.*

Yes, Shirley will walk, but what about her eyes? Things in the distance are getting fuzzy, but she won't tell anybody, especially not her mother, who gets frantic so easily. Her father couldn't care less that he is nearsighted and needs thick lenses. Patty has worn glasses for a year, the tortoiseshell, cat's-eye style that secured her place as the prettiest girl in school. Patty was elated by her trips to S. Galeski, the optical shop in downtown Richmond, reporting details of the exam, the doctor's care indicating that hers was a special case of vision compromised in a highly unusual way. She reported his assistant's approval when she chose the cat's-eye frames. With sharp new attention, as if Patty were a grown woman, teachers had commented on the glasses.

It was okay for Patty to announce things were getting blurred, yet Shirley is ashamed and embarrassed. Her failing vision feels like a flaw and a weakness. To read the blackboard, she goes to the front of the class, wondering why the teacher doesn't realize she can't see worth a dern anymore. At home, she can't see the TV screen clearly. With her sisters, she repeats earnest, exclamatory lines overheard from the shows their parents watch, lines that seem hilarious. *Perry Mason* is her parents' favorite, its music stern as an interrogation.

If she pulls one eye to the side, she sees a little better. What if she's going blind? That's her real fear, that this is not just something that could be fixed by borrowing Patty's glasses, which make everything look better, though slanted and slick, like looking through a wet windshield. Lately, by day's end, she's exhausted from trying to see.

Here comes her sister Diana, a first grader, clambering aboard the bus, chattering with a friend, eating an orange. Diana always smells of oranges. They take seats up front. Patty plops down beside Shirley and says, "Hey, how'd you get that? Do you know whose that *is?*"

Patty reaches for the prize on Shirley's lap, Ray West's lunch box, but Shirley won't let go, not even when Patty commands, "Let me *have* it."

Shirley alone will know the joy of its contents, will open it in her room and treasure the crumpled waxed paper and fading smells of tuna sandwiches and potato chips. She will uncap the Thermos, preparing herself for the fact that the glass lining probably shattered when it fell on the blacktop. The Thermos has a navy-blue top. Ray has drunk from that plastic top many times. His lips have touched it. Shirley will never let Patty get her hands on it.

The driver closes the door, and the bus proceeds with slow, stately motion. It glides onto Old Washington Highway, turns onto Mountain Road, and, within moments, reaches the Lloyds' front yard, the familiar mailbox and the stretch of grass and driveway. Shirley leaps off the bus ahead of Patty and Diana. She outruns Patty up the driveway and reaches the safety of her room.

There she hides the lunch box under her bed, where it remains like a forgotten dream for several days, days in which Shirley attempts to walk to school on her own. Alarmed, her parents cut short this plan, stopping her at the door. Shirley finds her voice: "I'm sick of being late." Her mother replies, "That hardly ever happens," and the family resumes its habits. Shirley can't stop getting up early and can't stop making the coffee, though she vows she'll never drink it and will be early everywhere she goes as a grownup, as early as she wants to be.

One day, she remembers the lunch box and opens it. It smells so bad she takes it outside, behind a little shed that was once a smokehouse. She sets it on top of weeds so tall and stiff their stalks barely bend beneath its weight. The Thermos isn't broken, but it smells so foul that Shirley's stomach shakes as she separates it into its parts and leaves it there.

For three days, a hard rain falls. When at last she ventures out to recover the lunch box and Thermos, a cloud of gnats rises from the wet, salty-smelling weeds. She dumps the rainwater, and liquid rust spills out. Where the astronaut's smile had been is a crater of red flakes, a death of what must be iron.

✦ ✦ ✦

THE old preacher at the Lloyds' church, an aged minister who was perfect except for his habit of checking his watch as soon as he stepped down from the pulpit ("as if he had someplace better to be," says Shirley's mother), has been sent to another church, and in his place is a new young preacher named Cal Mims.

Reverend Cal brings a guitar and sings in church. To Shirley's horror, he actually cries, voice breaking, face a shining waterfall as he talks about Vietnam. No, he hasn't been there, and he doesn't blame the draft dodgers. He lets it be known that the ministry is but one of many callings for him. Bartending, auto repair, truck driving—he has had stints in all these things.

Cal Mims's influence is felt in the Lloyds' home. Diana struggles to say a word that fascinates her and Shirley, a word from TV and now from the pulpit: *Vietnamese.*

"Viet-ma-nese," is the closest Diana gets.

The congregation splits in two, for Cal Mims or against him. He is too new, too young, too ready with tears and songs.

Each Sunday after the service, he and his wife make their way to the door of the sanctuary, where they stop, grab each other, and kiss. It's a long smooch that Shirley and her sisters wait for, while their mother frowns and their father studies his bulletin.

The old preacher, who checked his watch as he completed the service, has been sent to Goochland County to serve at a country church with outhouses in the backyard and no money for new plumbing or even paint. There is a report that he batted a wasps' nest from the eaves and almost died from the hundreds of stings he endured as the insects swarmed out. Among the congregation he left behind, particularly the anti-Cal sector, sympathy rises to a high tide. He was too old to be up on a ladder. Where were the young men who should have used gasoline and their own wits against the wasps? The nest develops its own legend: it was fifty years old, big as a bush.

Shirley overhears church members debating the advisability of asking the venerable preacher for advice about Cal Mims. There is the matter of the elderly minister's stunginess, the possibility that talk of dissent, any talk of Cal Mims, might tip the old gentleman—hospitalized now, bursting with histamine and blistered with welts—into shock and death. Shirley wonders if she and her mother are the only people who noticed he checked his watch. Maybe he is simply conscious of time, like Shirley herself.

"If his wife were still alive," her mother says, "she'd have made him stop that."

In this way, she pardons the old man, who never knew that he and his watch had offended.

Reverend Cal never wears a watch. Sometimes, if he gets caught up in his guitar music, the service lasts way over an hour. Other times, he'll finish early and invite people to come to his house for a cookout.

"Bring hot dogs!" his wife cries. "We've got plenty buns, but y'all bring your own meat."

Shirley and her family do not go to the cookouts.

"I have no intention," her mother murmurs, tight-lipped, on their way out to the car.

Reverend Cal has a daughter, Amanda, who is Shirley's age and who goes by a nickname, Manda. Manda Mims has beautiful blonde hair and bad teeth, curved and thin, as yellow as honeysuckle blossoms. Manda takes charge of the playground, and other children do her bidding. She trips Shirley and laughs when she falls. Manda boasts that at her last school, she was the star of the Christmas play. She strikes a pose and delivers "O Holy Night" in a piercing soprano: *Fall* on your *knees,* O *hear* the angel *voices.* When boys clownishly fall, Manda's followers fly at them, skirmishing, picking half a dozen small fights over which Manda presides, exultant.

Manda makes a play for Ray West, sitting boldly beside him in the cafeteria. At first, he picks up his tray and moves away. She persists, bribing him with Pop-Tarts. It works. He lets her sit with him, though he ignores her. Manda beams at him, sucking on her teeth as he licks jam from his fingers, his ears reddening. Shirley is ashamed for how easily he was corrupted.

Ever since school started in September, Shirley has waited for Field Day, waited with electric anticipation. Field Day. The very words are a summons, a setting free. It's been a fast spring, with trees leafing out and flowers tumbling over each other. There's one cold weekend just before the peonies bloom, and then the heat begins in earnest, a vivid, bee-buzzing warmth, full of the promise of every summer of her life, those she has lived and those future summers when she imagines herself on her own, leaving a beautiful office building at the end of a work day and strolling along a glamorous Richmond avenue. Even as she scuffs her shoes in the grass of a Glen Allen field, nine miles from downtown, she senses the city changing. Her mother grew up just down the street from an Old Soldiers' Home. Her mother actually saw Civil War veterans: "They were just real old," she says, "and then they were gone."

But Field Day is coming, and Shirley has little time for nostalgia. She's small and thin, but she can run—a matchstick hurtling through space. There's no other sport she's good at, not dodgeball or kickball, the two great games of her generation. Field Day means the students get to wear shorts, and regular instruction ends at lunchtime. Events will be held in a big meadow behind the school. The janitor will mow the field the day before, and its scent of fresh grass, weeds, sunshine, and wildflowers will ride the air all over Glen Allen.

Shirley is fast, yet nobody notices. For weeks, there has been practice at recess, although the playground distances aren't nearly as great as they will be in the big field. Often, she wins, or nearly wins, but everybody seems to be looking away when she crosses the finish line. That's all right. If on Field Day she drops the baton in the relay, they won't expect otherwise.

Manda Mims announces she will win. She tucks her head down and braces herself with one leg stretched back as she waits her turn in a relay, honeysuckle teeth bared.

Teachers indulge Manda and defer to her. It's not because she is a preacher's daughter. Cathy Jamison's father is the preacher at Glen Allen Baptist, but Cathy is quiet, and the teachers pay her no mind. Manda talks back and rolls her eyes. She orders other children into rough games that test their obedience to her. She blows pink bubbles that go *pok* when she snaps them, and teachers pretend she isn't chewing gum. She ruins Cathy Jamison's reputation by spreading a story that Cathy wet her pants at the movies, though everybody knows it isn't true.

Several of the younger teachers make excuses for Manda.

"Madcap," they say, smiling uneasily, mentioning a movie which is playing at the theater where Cathy Jamison supposedly disgraced herself, a show about a brother and sister who trade quips, get into scrapes, and catch spies, all without their parents. Shirley saw posters for the movie when she was downtown with her grandmother, Zee-Zee, and hated the madcap siblings on sight.

Shirley's vision is worse than ever. By Field Day, she'll be running blind. Lights of any kind sprout haloes and pulse when she looks at them. *This can't go on* is a phrase that runs through her mind, in a chastising voice from her mother's soap operas.

Suddenly the month of May ends, and Field Day arrives. By tradition, the afternoon begins with a game of red rover, the third, fourth, fifth, and sixth graders pitted against each other in equal numbers. Sprints and relays will come later. Shirley is shocked when her teacher calls her name, sending her into the red rover lineup. What is the point of sending a matchstick into battle? There are plenty of bigger, stronger students. Patty is put on the same team. Patty is sturdy. She just dislikes running.

Thank goodness they're on the same side. Shirley finds Patty and stands beside her, clutching her hand until Patty yelps, "Not so hard." One of Patty's friends takes Shirley's other hand. *I'll always be grateful to you for that,* Shirley imagines telling the girl, though she never does. As she faces the line of opponents across the field, her heart beats so hard, it feels like something's eating her from the inside.

Why did she ever look forward to this day?

Of all the games, she hates this one the most. A runner who fails to break through the opposing line must join the enemy. If you do break through, you take somebody back to your side. That is how red rover is won, by the claiming of foes who then must fight alongside you. There are few situations more terrifying than to be left on a sparse losing team, facing a huge army near the end of one of these battles. More than once, Shirley has simply let go of the hands holding hers, allowing an onrushing adversary to sail through empty space.

The cry comes: "Red rover, red rover, send Shirley on over!"

She freezes, her head roaring. Patty swings toward her, incredulous, her jaw snapping open so Shirley glimpses the rugged, shell-colored molars in the back of her mouth. Patty would run for her, would pretend it was her own name they called. All Shirley has to do is whisper, *You go,* and Patty will launch out across the field, holding her hands up to her chest the way girls do at her age, pushing the air away.

But it's Shirley's run, Shirley's fight. She won't shove it off on Patty, but she needs help.

"Your glasses," she says.

Patty whips them off and hands them over, and Shirley mashes them onto her own face. They're wide and wobbly, but she can see a sharper, if slanted, version of the field.

She hurls herself forward, faster than fire. She will never understand why they called her first. Small, weak children are left for last. They bounce off the human chain like a ball against a concrete wall and are absorbed into the enemy camp. In a few more seconds, humiliated, she will have to take her place at the end of that long line stretching almost to the woods, fighting off mosquitoes, for the grass is high there. Who called her name? She'll never know. Had it not been for Patty's stricken face, she might believe she heard wrong.

As she crosses that no-man's-land, the thought comes to her that she could veer away and run right off the field. Her mother is here somewhere, in the small crowd of mothers who have brought Kool-Aid and cookies to be enjoyed later. Ray West has bragged that his mother brought Keebler pecan sandies. Shirley doesn't want pecan sandies or even her mother's arms. She wants her own house, its cool emptiness scented with the bacon and canned peaches her family ate for breakfast, the electric clock over the stove humming its faint insect-like song. She could run home and reach her own porch, gather up the cats, and take them all inside.

But she cannonballs toward the enemy line, hearing a hard wild yell that she barely recognizes as her own, seeing with amazement the terrified faces coming into focus, boys' and girls' mouths open, bodies stiffening as they prepare for her extraordinary momentum. Are some of them crying, their panicked sobs echoing into the trees? Why isn't this game against the law?

She couldn't stop if she wanted to. She plows into the line, breaking through, the borrowed glasses flying off her face as she strikes Ray's chest. She knocks Ray down as if he's cardboard. Grassy ground rises up as she pitches forward, one ankle locked around Ray's knee. She can claim him, grab his arm and run him back across the field, a prize she has bought with all her strength.

But the ground is still coming up at her, and there is a rock in the dirt, a rock that strikes her on the temple, and she is dizzy. She lies still. There will be no return trip across the field, no relays or sprints, only a visit to the doctor for stitches in her head. Lying on the grass, she knows what else is to come: luminous lenses of her own from S. Galeski, the prismatic bending of light through glass, the precision with which the optician will adjust the frames with his powder-white palms. Patty will need new glasses, too. Hers are driven deeply into the ground, smashed and ruined. Later, Shirley and Patty will examine them in shared astonishment: so much damage wrought in an instant, as if from a lightning strike.

None of this will feel like Shirley's choice, but in hooking her foot around Ray's leg, in falling to earth, she has already given in. *I didn't know it was you,* she wants to tell him, to set this straight once and for all. *I didn't realize who you were until I was right on top of you.*

Even Manda Mims would not have dared crash into Ray West in front of the whole world. Of all the girls who throw themselves at him, Shirley is the only one who didn't mean to. Ten years from now, she might say that to him as a joke, believing he would remember this day, this catastrophe. All her life, it will amaze her that not everybody remembers the same details she does, that not all intimacy leaves a mark.

Around her, red rover is in chaos, but she is safe on the ground, her bruised face swelling, her blood strawberry-sweet on her tongue. She longs to tell all of this to the old, stung preacher. She will wait until her family is out of the house on some warm, sleepy afternoon, and then she'll pick up the phone and tell him about her run, her fall. She'll hear in the receiver the drone of a thousand wasps closing in on that other fallen one, their stingers punching endlessly through skin.

+ + +

IT'S June, and school is ending. The teachers are losing their grip, losing their minds. One moment, Mrs. Maycomb, Shirley's teacher, speaks reverently of masking tape—Shirley will never know another individual who finds so many occasions to talk about masking tape—and moves her hands over the classroom globe as if the sphere is heaven. A moment later, she's fire and fury, scolding poor little Tilma Harrell, who cries when she can't find her pencil or her sweater: "Tilma, if you don't stop that sniffling, I'll give you something to cry *about.*"

Tilma can't stop. Her sobs run down the classroom walls like niter, whatever that is, something in the Edgar Allan Poe stories Shirley reads. It's not a lost sweater, Shirley wants to tell Mrs. Maycomb, it's despair. Shirley has seen Tilma's mother contemplating bread at the store with a look of a hundred lost sweaters. Wonder Bread, who eats it? It's too expensive. Only Ray West eats Wonder Bread. With her new glasses, Shirley can not only see the colorful circles on bread wrappers, she can read a list of ingredients from practically across a room.

To shut down Tilma's snuffling, Mrs. Maycomb raises her arm and snaps her fingers, a signal that all the children should do the same, to create that precious thing called quiet, the commodity that teachers value supremely. Raise your arm and snap your fingers, but only once, until the whole room is a sea of raised arms. One by one, arms rise. Even Tilma Harrell's arm is in the air, drained and bloodless. There will come a day, Shirley knows, when Mrs. Maycomb makes this motion for the last time. Mrs. Maycomb on her deathbed will raise her arm and snap her fingers, and God will answer her with the quiet that she loves.

One morning, Ray West brings in a tape recorder, sleek and oblong in a special case, and the whole class records their voices.

"Say something important," Mrs. Maycomb commands.

What is important enough?

"My brother and me," says Ray, "we like to laugh," and he laughs a Halloween laugh into the microphone and plays it back, "Mwah-ha-ha," and everybody wants to do that.

At recess, Ray takes the tape recorder outside, and there are some dirty things said on it by the toughest boys. Mrs. Maycomb, getting wind of this talk, takes the tape recorder away, even dumps out the batteries, and locks it up in her desk, her face a picture of condemnation.

Summer will come, and then it will be a long, glorious time until Shirley starts checking the mailbox for the postcard that bears the name of her new teacher. That is how teachers begin, as names on postcards, showing up one August morning in the mailbox. She has seen Patty hop with delight or howl with anguish at a name on a card. All the teachers are legendary, young or old, married or old maids. The school's two men, principal and janitor, are famous too, as are the cafeteria ladies. What could be mightier than the control of lunch? Shirley wonders who gets to think up the menus. Her mother says it's probably a dietitian in an office in Richmond, jotting down the combinations: Sloppy Joes and applesauce; fishwiches and chopped kale, which nobody eats except the teachers, dutifully setting an example: *Greens are good for you;* chili con carne and fruit cocktail. When Shirley's favorite meal is served—fried chicken, mashed potatoes and gravy, canned snaps, and a plain sheet cake—she longs to thank the dietitian. Is that worthy authority sorry when the school year ends? In her kitchen, which is surely near the Capitol, she can close the bin where cartons of milk are kept for all the children in Virginia—a nickel for plain, six cents for chocolate—and retreat to the clean, hushed kitchen of her head, all stainless steel with puddles of disinfectant drying on the floor.

Ray West, having lost his lunch box, buys his lunch every day for the rest of the year. Shirley wonders if he misses the lunch box and if Mrs. Maycomb ever gave the tape recorder back to him. She'll still be wondering about these things when she's as old as her grandmother ZeeZee and her friends, stylish widows who discuss food with zeal and fear. There is something called diverticulitis that inspires them to violent talk about blueberries and tomatoes, revealing a frenzy just beneath the surface of their lives: "Don't eat anything with seeds!" *Diverticulitis* sounds like something that could drag an old lady away screaming, clutching for wig, smock, salad fork, black shoes, dark thoughts.

Shirley thinks about old people a lot, and worries about them. Are there really some who are so poor they live off cat food? She has heard about that. She's not sure she believes it, yet at the Glen Allen store, a small grocery shop, she lingers in the pet food aisle to examine the old folks browsing there. Diverticulitis seems like nothing, compared to eating cat food. Nothing smells worse than canned cat food, though cats love it. If you're really starving, or if you've got a lot of dogs, you can buy the great big sacks of dog chow that are for sale outside the store, the bags stacked high like mattresses. Sometimes Shirley and her sisters, bored while their mother shops, climb up on the bags. Train tracks lie across from the store, and when trains roll by, Shirley feels she is swimming with the motion of the great swaying hoppers. She and Patty and Diana stretch out on the lumpy bags and wave to the man in the caboose, who is just a glimpse of a tanned face and a blue-striped, waving arm. They smell the meaty, mealy kibble in the thick paper bags and the dusty, sneezy daisies that grow wild beside the parking lot, and it's almost as if summer has already started.

✦   ✦   ✦

THE last day of school feels like the seasons are all mixed up. It's June, but cool and rainy, with a rising wind. There's pizza for lunch, the thick, cheesy squares cold in the middle. Manda Mims makes a show of giving her piece to Ray West, who accepts it matter-of-factly, then looks around the table with a grin like the one he gave when he was chased and cornered.

"Last night," he says, "my brother proposed to this girl. They were at a restaurant. He got the manager to put him on the loudspeaker, and he popped the question."

A crowd gathers at Ray's table to hear this. His brother David is eighteen. Long ago, as a sixth grader in this very building, David West organized a book drop so stupendous that people still talk about it. The entire sixth grade dropped books on the floor at the very same second, making a sound so loud you could hear it outside the building. The principal called a special PTA meeting to make sure such a thing never happened again. Parents still go tight-lipped about the book drop. Shirley never tires of picturing all those students with their heaviest books at the edge of the desks, watching the clock above the blackboard.

Ray grins about the proposal, stretching out his story.

"It was a joke," he says. "They've done it at other places, him and that girl."

"Why?" Shirley asks.

Manda Mims crinkles her eyes, merrily tonguing her honeysuckle teeth. All is well in Manda's world. The church has voted to keep her father. It turned into a love feast, Shirley heard. The Lloyd family wasn't there, having stayed home because Diana had a cold. When the votes were counted and results announced, Reverend Cal cried. His wife hugged everybody, and Manda played the organ, really just banged on it, but nobody stopped her. Cakes were brought out and coffee readied in the church kitchen, indicating that people had hatched this jubilee in advance, which to Shirley's mother proved the voting process was fraudulent. The celebration was capped off by a gift certificate for Reverend Cal. Money had been collected, and a delegation had gone downtown to a music store to purchase the certificate, rumored to exceed two hundred dollars. Shirley's mother groaned when she heard all this and said, *Well, some people just won't go back now.* Was there anything written on the cakes? she wanted to know, and her informer, a family cousin who took the maddening stance of just reporting the events and not condemning the Mimses, said come to think of it, yes. A big coconut cake said in blue letters, We love you, Cal. *Then fine,* said Shirley's mother, *we'll find another church.* The cousin said, *Oh, Jean, don't be so hasty.*

"Why did they do that?" Shirley asks Ray. "Why did they act like they're getting married, if they're not?"

"Free meal," Ray says, spreading his arms. "The manager always does that. People clap when the girl says yes. They had hamburger platters, plus ice cream sundaes. The manager said their names on the loudspeaker. They gave made-up names."

How many times can you give fake names, eat free, and get away with it? *Don't,* Shirley wants to tell Ray's brother and the girl, *don't do that.* In her mind, they laugh and touch hands across the table, and Shirley sees it will always be this way, she can't stop it. She doesn't question how smoothly Ray used the word *proposed.* All of them know the importance of words like that. Girls learn serious clothing terms from playing dolls: *cummerbund, tuxedo.* A doll's cummerbund, like a real man's, is wine-red and silky, girdling his waist over a white dress shirt and black pants. Someday, Ray West will slip on fancy clothes and go out to eat in a restaurant with a woman. Girls his age, smoothing the tiny tucks of a doll's formalwear, are preparing him.

Shirley catches Tilma Harrell's eye. Tilma is all agog. *Loudspeaker* and *platters* did it.

"How long did people clap?" Shirley asks.

"A long time," Ray says, "and they kept coming over to congratulate him."

"Did he kiss her?" Manda asks. She raises her chin at Ray and sucks her teeth.

"Yeah," and the table goes wild, he says it so easy.

II

SUMMER OF LOVE

July 1967

At Vacation Bible School, Shirley's class produces the ugliest art projects she has ever seen—praying hands made of plaster of Paris. The teacher, a young woman named Ginger Ficklin, does all the mixing of plaster and the casting herself. She narrates the process, and the children watch restlessly, batting at a fly that circles the room.

Then they have to wait for the plaster to dry.

The fly lands on Shirley's arm. She shoos it away, and it goes to explore the pink part in Tilma Harrell's white-blonde hair. Tilma is the tiniest person in the class. Shirley is little too, and glad she's not *that* tiny. The only living thing in the room that is tinier than Tilma Harrell is the fly on Tilma's head.

At last the praying hands are dried out and unmolded. Ginger Ficklin does all of that, too, while she talks about the place of art in society. She covers a table with newspaper and lines up the hands, each pair vertical and clasped and larger than life.

"There," she says. "Now you get to paint them black or gold."

Gold is fancier, but black is more dramatic. Shirley hates the praying hands. The whole project casts a pall. She gives in to dread, to gloom, and chooses the black paint. Lots of the children are choosing black, a choice Ginger Ficklin seems to approve of. The grooved plaster fingernails and knuckles look horribly real, reminding Shirley of a picture in the *National Geographic* of a body found in a peat bog. The hands create deep terror in Shirley's heart.

She takes her praying hands home and smashes them against the radiator in her room. They shatter easily, blasting noisily apart. The white plaster shows through the black paint like bone. She feels worse, as if she has killed the pitiful, curled-up peat man once and for all.

Even when she cleans up the mess and puts it in the trash, there's no sense of relief. Vacation Bible School is lasting so long. Because of the heat, midmorning recess is usually canceled. The other groups are in the doldrums too, according to Shirley's sisters. Diana's class is gluing paper crosses onto felt bookmarks. Patty's class planted seeds in little pots while their teacher, a bewigged ancient, fell asleep at her desk.

"All the boys dropped out at snack time," Patty complains at the supper table.

Few boys are left in Bible school by Patty's age anyway, and they are babyfied creatures whose mothers still pick out their clothes every night. Ray West, of course, is the opposite of that. Though his family belongs to the church, he is not attending Bible school this year. Shirley misses him.

The Lloyds are in church limbo. Cal Mims is anathema to Shirley's mother, but she has decreed that Bible school is still acceptable for Shirley and her sisters.

Shirley doesn't tell her mother that Reverend Cal, with newly shaggy hair and tiny glasses, stops by her class every day. Is it because Shirley and her classmates are Manda's age? Or because the teacher is pretty? Manda and her mother are at Expo '67 in Montreal, Canada. To Manda's classmates, Cal describes Manda's phone calls, the exhibits she has seen, and the rides she has enjoyed.

The plaster of Paris has created a lingering, damp, basement odor in the classroom. Shirley listens dutifully, her head down, as Cal addresses the group. Manda and her mother had to go through Customs, Shirley learns, whatever Customs is, and her mother got all nervous at the question *Where were you born?* and for a moment she couldn't remember, Cal says. Then Manda saved the day by saying, *My mom was born in Peoria, Illinois.* He pronounces it "Illinoise." Shirley's mother would really groan at that. So Manda's mother is from Illinois, never mind that she says "y'all."

Cal Mims makes Shirley nervous. Just being around him feels dangerous. She fears he will take her aside and ask why her family has stopped coming to church.

Yet she dares to say, "How come you didn't you go to Expo '67, too?"

He is sitting with the children and the teacher in a circle of chairs. In a picture on the wall, Jesus's expression reminds Shirley of a sleepy cat. His hair waves above his forehead, the color rich enough to illustrate a box of dye. Shirley's mother lately pauses by hair dye at the grocery store. She'll pick up a box, sigh, and set it back on the shelf. The store stocks only a few colors, and anybody who goes near that rack is scrutinized by employees and other shoppers.

Shirley's question apparently rattles Cal Mims.

"Why didn't I go to Expo '67?" he says. "Because I have to work. When I'm not doing church stuff, I paint houses. Frankly, I'm overdue for a raise. Would you tell your parents that for me, kids?" He pushes his tiny glasses up his nose. "My in-laws are paying for this trip. It's costing a bundle."

"Oh," murmurs Shirley, humiliated.

Everybody knows about the house painting he does for extra money, but it is news to Shirley that he is mad about it and feels poor. Her mother has taught her never to ask people about their finances.

Today, Cal Mims has word of something even more important than Manda's vacation.

"People, I'm here to inform you that someone you know has been drafted."

Shirley's mind snags on *people.* Younger teachers use it when they want the students to like them. Dignified, established teachers never stoop to *people.* They use *boys and girls,* or sometimes *class.*

Then the full import of Cal Mims's words reaches Shirley. He must be talking about himself. He'll have to go fight the Viet-ma-nese. Maybe the old preacher can come back. She looks up hopefully.

"David West has been drafted," Cal says. "Do you kids know what that means?"

David West, of course, is Ray's dashing eighteen-year-old brother, engineer of book drops and proposer of false marriages.

Tilma Harrell shakes her head, her thin white hair flipping onto her cheeks. Of course Tilma wouldn't know what *drafted* means. Cal Mims looks pleased.

"It's okay not to know," he says, and Shirley realizes they're in trouble now. They might be here all day. "This is different from World War Two. Your dads fought in World War Two, right?"

Shirley's classmates nod, and she does too, proudly.

"The war in Vietnam," Cal says, "is not like World War Two. This time, we ought not to think about enemies. We should think about love. I say so to you, and I'd say the same thing to LBJ."

He is slipping into pulpit mode. Ginger Ficklin, who just graduated from college and who is, in the expressed opinion of Shirley's mother, right skittish and flighty to be teaching Bible school, regards him adoringly. She has told the children to call her Ginger, not Miss Ficklin, something Shirley can't bring herself to do. All the boys are in love with Ginger Ficklin, who has ginger-colored hair, gingery eyelashes that she bats at Cal Mims, and gingery lips that smile in a bow. She looks like she wants to clap for him. Shirley's third-grade teacher, Mrs. Maycomb, would not allow Cal Mims to monopolize Vacation Bible School, would politely manage to *move things along*, a phrase adults are fond of, would move things along so Cal Mims would be out the door, David West or no David West.

"My dad says we ought not to be over there," pipes up Tim Thornton, a wiry boy with stick-out ears.

"That's right," Cal says. "Does your dad say why?"

"He says we're in a war we can't win," Tim Thornton says.

Tim Thornton rises in Shirley's estimation, despite the fact he was once sent to the principal's office for making the titty gesture when talk at the lunch table turned to bras: he held out his shirt with his fingertips.

"Plus, my dad hates gooks," he adds.

Everybody waits to see what Cal Mims will say. Ginger Ficklin waits, holding her breath so her chest sticks out. If Tim Thornton notices and wants to make the titty gesture, he resists. Cal's cutoff jeans are tight. He's getting fat. Even his feet, in green flip-flops, look fat.

"Let's not call the Vietnamese names, okay, pal?" he says. "But your dad's right about a war we can't win, and there's another factor, several other factors."

Shirley wants to get up and run. Yet everybody else, and certainly Ginger Ficklin, is attentive. Except for Tilma Harrell, who is biting her fingernails. *That child looks like she needs to drink some milk and eat some meat,* Shirley's mother always says, and follows up with a question: *Can Tilma tell time yet, or does she still talk about the big hand and the little hand?*

"Being drafted means you're a dead duck, people," Cal says. Shirley has to admit that so far, what he is saying matches up pretty well with her parents' views. "The Vietnamese are smart. Their culture is probably more advanced than ours. And you know what? Maybe communism is okay after all."

This is not what Shirley's parents are saying. Communists force people to do things. You don't have any choices, and you would always be poor. The only good thing communists have done is to produce the glamorous Svetlana, daughter of a Russian big shot. Svetlana escaped from Russia, and her picture is showing up in the newspapers. Shirley and her mother love to say her name. Svetlana looks so fashionable in turtleneck sweaters with her hair like a wing across her forehead. *What color do you think her sweater is?* Shirley's mother has asked as they look at newspaper pictures, and Shirley said, *Red.*

"My dad hates commies," Tim Thornton blurts. "He says they oughta go to hell."

Cal Mims ignores this. "Just this morning, I met with the West family and prayed with them. David has to report to training camp, and then he'll be shipped out. There's a good chance he'll be killed."

Tilma Harrell yanks her fingernails out of her mouth and bursts into tears. Shirley hopes this will put an end to the whole talk, that Cal Mims will be embarrassed enough to leave, but instead, Ginger Ficklin gets up, goes to the desk where she keeps a knapsack, and brings forth a bottle which she uncaps and hands to Tilma. The liquid makes a fizzy sound.

"Ginger beer," she stage-whispers. "Drink it. It'll calm you down. It's not really beer."

Oh, this is too much. Ginger Ficklin and ginger beer. Everybody will want ginger beer now, will pester their mothers to find it and buy it. Tilma sips the suds intently, like a bird pecking for worms, then leans her head back and drains the bottle, tears gone.

Cal Mims is talking about body bags. Shirley tries to tune him out.

"Kids your age are being hit by napalm," he says. "Burned alive."

Now it's Ginger Ficklin who is crying. Her shoulders shake, her gingery hair quivers. Shirley bets she wishes she hadn't given away her ginger beer. Cal Mims stands up, crosses the circle, and hands her a paint-covered handkerchief, a *snot rag* in anybody's lingo, but she accepts it, blows her nose on it, and looks up at him tremulously, with swimming eyes.

"That's what I can't bear to think about," she chokes out. "The children."

Cal places a hand on her shoulder.

"We could stick our heads in the sand. Or," he says, and pauses.

Shirley can't believe her eyes. Ginger Ficklin is leaning her cheek against Cal Mims's hand. Nobody answers the "or," though Cal appears to be waiting for a response. Tilma Harrell, crossing and uncrossing her legs, needs to pee bad, Shirley guesses, and who wouldn't, after drinking a whole bottle of ginger beer. Cal Mims is taking up the whole morning. Snack time came and went. Everybody has to pee, Shirley included.

"Or we can make ourselves heard," Cal declares.

He's actually caressing Ginger Ficklin's cheek, right in front of everybody, and she's snuggling against his hand, eyes closed.

This, after all, is the Summer of Love. Shirley has heard about the Summer of Love on the news, has read about it in the *Richmond Times-Dispatch*. It has to do with rock music and long hair. Cal Mims must be part of it, although the Summer of Love doesn't apply to the Viet-ma-nese or to colored people either, judging from other things in the news, like the race riots in Buffalo, New York, where black people were clubbed by the police.

She wonders if black kids go to Vacation Bible School. They probably do. They're probably having their snacks and working on art projects right this minute, unless a colored version of Cal Mims is fussing at them about war.

"David West's mother was talking about sending him somewhere the U.S. government can't find him, like Canada," Cal says, and Shirley is sure David's mother wouldn't want everybody knowing this.

Cal's hand wanders away from Ginger Ficklin's cheek, and he ambles back to his seat and plops down. Shirley looks longingly toward the closed door. It's hot in the room. Her glasses are steaming up. So are Cal Mims's wire-rimmed ones. He takes them off and rubs the lenses with his paint-splattered shirt, lifting it up and stretching it out so far that everybody can see his belly button and tufts of hair surrounding the belly button. Ginger Ficklin sees it all. Shirley sees her see. Ginger looks at his navel so bug-eyed you'd think it was talking to her.

"I'm organizing a bus trip to Washington, DC," he says. "A demonstration."

Shirley's parents have promised that someday they will take her and her sisters to Washington, DC, and they'll go to the National Zoo. Maybe that's all Cal Mims will do, take the bus to the zoo and talk about the war on the way up. Maybe Shirley can get her parents' permission to go. Her whole family could go, as long as they don't have to sit near him.

"I'm going all the way to the White House," he says, "all the way to the Capitol steps, and you're invited. Everyone can go. We might need two buses, or even more."

He is looking right at Shirley. This is a challenge to her, to the Lloyd family. Her mother will be furious. *Getting children all worked up.* Shirley knows her parents won't go on this trip, though her mother might admit, *I'd like to be a fly on the wall,* meaning, she'd love to see Cal Mims make an idiot of himself in Washington, DC.

"Have you ever seen a demonstration, Shirley?" he asks.

"On TV," she says faintly. It's awful to be singled out.

"It's a lot better in person," he says. "We'll have banners and signs, and we can dress so we'll be noticed."

"I have an idea," Ginger Ficklin says. "Tie-dyeing! I'll bring my tie-dyeing supplies tomorrow. Everybody, bring a white T-shirt and Rit dye."

"What kind of bus will it be?" Tim Thornton asks. "A school bus?"

"A charter bus," Cal Mims replies, and the room is electrified. That sounds like the city buses that Shirley rides with ZeeZee, downtown.

"Tell your parents to protest," he says, "to rise up against the inhuman slaughter . . ." His voice trails off, and Shirley realizes this is a rehearsed speech. He must have practiced in front of a mirror, without even Manda or *Y'all bring your own meat* as an audience. "Let's all go," he concludes.

"I wanna go," cries Tim Thornton.

"Me too," others yelp, and Cal Mims smiles.

"Well, I'm hungry," he says, and Shirley hopes escape is near. "It must be time for lunch. Do y'all eat here?"

So even though he's the preacher, he doesn't know the Bible school schedule. Bible school ends before lunch, and everybody goes home. He's dumber than Shirley thought.

Other classes are letting out. The hallway fills with jostling and calling.

"That's all for today, kids," Ginger Ficklin says. "See you tomorrow. Bring your white T-shirts," as if everybody has white T-shirts at home just waiting to be tie-dyed. Shirley doesn't have one and doesn't know where she'll get one.

Tim Thornton opens the door, and fresh air gusts in, even if it's just hallway air. Tilma Harrell is the first one out, a trapped white rat let loose. The classroom empties, but Cal Mims and Ginger Ficklin remain. Shirley stays in the hallway, attuned to their silence.

"Want to go grab a burger?" Cal asks at last.

"Sure," Ginger Ficklin says, "and let's get ice cream." Her laughter is a tinkle.

Shirley leans as close to the doorway as she dares, but they don't see her. They only see each other. Holding Ginger's gaze, Cal picks at the hem of his cutoffs, tearing out a thread that he flicks to the floor.

"So how'd I do?" he asks.

"You were great, Cal. You were fabulous. Did you bring your guitar?"

"Sure did, babe. It's out in the car."

✦   ✦   ✦

HAVING rejected Cal Mims, the Lloyds make a few forays to the church in Goochland County, which was so briefly and recently the seat of the old preacher. A seminary student now occupies the pulpit, his Adam's apple jumping. Shirley can tell he's afraid to be up there. People cup their ears to hear his faint voice, then make much over him when the service is over. They make much over the Lloyds, too, clearly hoping to recruit new members, gratified by the news of the Mims-inspired controversy that has worked to their benefit, for not only the Lloyds but several other disaffected families now attend the country church, and there are plans to build an addition with modern restrooms. Shirley decides not to mind the privies. There are separate outhouses for men and women. The women's is clean and has a vase of flowers on a little table. Inside the church, there is a sink, at least, where you can wash your hands.

Later, her mother says, "It's just so far away, that church."

But the distance has an advantage. It means they sometimes stop for lunch at a hamburger stand out in the country, an enterprise operated by a family that, like the Lloyds, owns many cats. The cats walk on the car while the Lloyds eat their meal at a picnic table.

"We could always go back to our old church," Shirley's father says.

"To Cal Mims?" says Shirley's mother, in the tone of incredulity in which she'd said *Vasco da Gama.*

"Maybe he'll be better," Shirley's father says, "now that he's had the vote of confidence."

"Well, he didn't get *my* vote," says her mother.

One Sunday at the Goochland church, the seminary student announces he has volunteered to go to Vietnam. He whips out a gun and a sword.

"There's a time for peace, and a time for war, and now is the time for war. I'm going to fight for my country."

The church empties fast, men and women and children rising from the pews and surging toward the door. Shirley finds herself laughing, yet she doesn't feel happy. Her mouth is open, and the sounds she makes are close to crying. Somebody steps on her heel, and it hurts.

"He's a nut," her mother says as they shakily eat hamburgers at the wayside stand.

"Oh, he's just young," her father says. "He was showing off." He flicks an ant from the picnic table.

"I don't know what's the matter with preachers these days," her mother says. "They used to be better." She returns sadly to the subject of the old, stung parson. "He might be the last of his kind." Pictures of odd zoo animals pop into Shirley's head, specimens now said to be extinct, in photographs from long ago. "We should go visit him," her mother says, but Shirley knows the old preacher will never be seen by her family again. He is as gone as the antique combatants at the soldiers' home, back in her mother's childhood.

"I hope he won't get hurt over there," her mother says of the seminary student.

"He doesn't know what he's getting himself into," her father says.

✦ ✦ ✦

IT'S a full-fledged scandal, the way Cal Mims and Ginger Ficklin carry on while Manda and her mother are at Expo '67. They swim together at the local pool, Overhill Lake, Ginger in a bikini, Cal leaping off the high dive. Then they depart in his car, going somewhere to take off their clothes, Shirley is sure of it, though she can't quite picture what will happen next.

He plays his guitar on the church steps when Bible school is over for the day, with Ginger at his feet, and they sing "All You Need Is Love."

Ray West shows up at Bible school one day and announces his brother has decided he *wants* to go to Vietnam, because war might be groovy.

"Maybe David'll get to fly his own chopper," Ray crows.

All the boys become helicopters, spinning around and whirling their arms, making loud mechanical sounds. Cal Mims regards them with hooded eyes and launches into "Incense and Peppermints." There's something odd about a father knowing all these songs, even if he is just Manda's father.

His hair now hangs to his shoulders. He swaggers when he walks, and on Sundays—the Lloyd family having resumed church attendance, frank curiosity on the part of Shirley's mother overmastering her dislike—Shirley observes that beneath his black robe, he wears sandals and jeans. Church attendance swells, doubles. Fascination with Cal Mims and Ginger Ficklin runs so high that people just can't stay away.

In the pulpit, he proclaims that the whole country is undergoing a revolution, "and music's a big part of it, people. Janis and Jimi and Joan, they're the heart and soul of the new America. You can be a Christian and be a hippie too."

Who are Janis, Jimi, and Joan, wonders Shirley, and why does it matter what they think?

"Don't forget about Jane Fonda," Cal says. "Who cares about her politics when she's such a good-looking gal?" He chuckles, then cups his ear. "I don't hear anybody laughing. Church doesn't have to be so serious."

At this, a few people in the congregation quietly rise and depart. The act of walking out, Shirley realizes, is part of the pleasure of the scandal, a way people can keep up with Cal Mims's doings yet show their disapproval.

"A revolution," Cal repeats, "a social and sexual revolution."

Patty digs her elbow into Shirley's ribs, meaning, Did you hear that? Shirley heard it, all right, *sexual* loud and clear. Their father is reading his bulletin; their mother's lips are pressed together. Ginger Ficklin is perched up in the next pew, wearing a pink shirtwaist dress that covers her knees. She's with her parents, baffled-looking folks with faded gingery hair who are probably the only ones in Glen Allen who don't know what's going on.

A few more members of the congregation rise and slip out of the sanctuary, thus missing Cal's announcement that his wife and daughter are having such a wonderful time that they've decided to extend the trip. Manda and her mother will fly from Montreal to New York City, where they will stay for four days and three nights, so "my musical Manda can see some Broadway shows."

So Cal Mims and Ginger Ficklin have four more days and three more nights to carry on, and *Y'all bring your own meat* will have a big fat surprise in store if she ever gets home.

"There can't be anything going on if they're so open about it," Shirley's father says as the family eats their Sunday dinner. "I think it's aboveboard, just like if I had lunch with, say, Mildred Hancock."

Shirley and her sisters roar with laughter. Mildred Hancock is his secretary, sixty years old and bearing no resemblance to Ginger Ficklin.

Though Mildred Hancock is a whiz at typing, she drives him crazy because she never stops talking. He has vowed that if he ever has the chance to recommend her for another job, he'll write her an outstanding reference, a plan that strikes Shirley as brilliant.

Shirley's mother flinches. "Do you and Mildred Hancock have lunch together, Merle?"

"No, I just said if," he protests. "*If* I did. No reason Cal Mims can't be friends with that young woman, what is her name?"

"It's not Dorothy," Shirley says.

Whenever he can't remember a woman's name, he thinks it's Dorothy. This is a joke among Shirley and her sisters.

"Ginger. Her name is Ginger Ficklin," her mother says, "and it's obvious they're more than friends. It's disgraceful."

"Well, I don't know about Ginger Ficklin, but anybody who has lunch with Mildred Hancock," her father says, "better be wearing earplugs," and he and Patty and Shirley and Diana laugh until they wheeze, but Shirley's mother does not join in.

It won't matter how much Manda Mims brags about Expo '67, Shirley realizes. It won't matter if she got room service every day in Montreal and New York too. Nobody will pay any attention to her, because they're all watching her father. Day after day, he sits right there on the church steps with Ginger Ficklin, twanging his guitar and singing "Ruby Tuesday," "I'm a Believer," "Kind of a Drag," and "Penny Lane." He's Mick Jagger, The Monkees, The Buckinghams, and The Beatles all in ten minutes. He's growing out his fingernails so he won't need a pick. The long, cracked nails horrify Shirley.

When he launches into "Happy Together," he looks at Ginger meaningfully, and a blush edges up her cheeks, all the way to her gingery eyelashes.

The kids who want to be cool stay after Bible school to sing with them, while their mothers wait at the curb in their cars. The mothers are open-mouthed. This is adultery and courtship all at once, sex and long fingernails all mixed up together, and this delay, this waiting in the hot cars, is messing up their whole day, because at home, the kids' lunches are ready and out on the table, and the moms are hungry too, yet here they are watching the preacher and the bombshell carry on.

The last day of Bible school, Tilma Harrell's mother, of all people, crosses the church yard to sit on the steps with Cal and Ginger, only she doesn't know the words to the songs the way they do, so she just sways to the music with her eyes closed.

"Is your mom sick?" Tim Thornton asks Tilma Harrell. "She looks like she don't feel good."

"I don't know," Tilma says, her rabbity face alarmed.

Tilma's mother is the tiniest grownup Shirley knows, almost as tiny as Tilma, and, like Tilma, she is all-white, hair and skin and probably her eyes too, all white except for the terrible tie-dyed, carnival-colored clothes she is affecting these days. She is going to Washington, DC, and is dragging Tilma with her, and they are not alone; there is a ground-swell of support for this excursion, which Cal Mims has announced will take place in August.

"Hey, Cal," Tilma's mother says. "How do you have time to learn so many songs?"

A bleat escapes from Tilma's mouth, an expression of pure terror, as if waiting for Cal Mims to smite her mother for this impudence.

"When I'm painting houses," he says, "I happen to listen to the radio." He and Ginger exchange a glance, and Ginger rewards him with a grin. Cal Mims turns his back on Tilma's mother, wipes sweat from his face, and says, "It's hot. The planet is thirsty. My tomato plants are dying. Anybody know a rain dance?"

He plucks deep chords, slow and then fast. Tilma's mother jumps up, hops around, and waves her arms at the sky. Ginger Ficklin and Cal Mims lean toward each other and laugh. The kids on the steps sing a high "Ahh" and pat their mouths to make Indian war cries, *wah-wah-wah.* Tilma's mother dances faster. Shirley has never seen a grownup act like that. She didn't know a grownup *could.* If Cal Mims can get a grown woman to do that, he's capable of anything. Everybody's laughing at Tilma's mother.

Tilma Harrell, a white mouse dashing for cover, bolts toward her mother's car. She climbs in and crouches on the floor so you can't see any of her, not even the top of her head.

+   +   +

"AND there's more," Shirley tells ZeeZee on the phone. "When Manda and her mother got back from Montreal and New York, Ginger Ficklin moved in with them."

Shirley's mother takes the phone from her. The scandal has reached such proportions that Shirley's mother says she doesn't want her daughters to know what is going on, although in fact she gets much of her information from them.

"The story is that the preacher is painting the Ficklins' house," Shirley's mother tells ZeeZee, who is following this saga from Richmond, nine miles away, though she has never met the participants. "Ginger's parents went somewhere," Shirley's mother says, "and Ginger, for whatever reason, didn't go with them. The Ficklins' house is empty, and *she* is over *there*." A pause, as if ZeeZee has asked a question, and Shirley's mother says, "Apparently it's perfectly all right with his wife. I've heard she even suggested it."

To Shirley's amazement, even more happens. Through the grocery store grapevine, she, her sisters, and their mother learn that as soon as Ginger Ficklin was installed in the Mimses' house, Manda, her suitcase barely unpacked from Broadway, was sent to visit cousins in Norfolk.

After the grocery store, Shirley, her sisters, and their mother head to Overhill Lake, where they find a cozy trio on display. Cal Mims, *Y'all bring your own meat,* and Ginger Ficklin are rubbing Coppertone on each other's backs, their beach towels overlapping.

"And they were all calling each other Babe," Shirley's mother reports to ZeeZee on the phone, while Shirley listens avidly. There's something exciting in hearing these dispatches, in knowing how shocked and righteously gratified ZeeZee is. Shirley's mother doesn't bother to lower her voice: "Babe and Babe and Babe. I want them gone."

How do Babe and Babe and Babe have so much time to sun and swim, if Reverend Babe is painting Ginger's parents' house? Shirley and her mother and sisters drive slowly by the Ficklins' dwelling, their mother not even offering an excuse about why they are on that street. Other cars too are inching past the gray frame house. Scaffolding surrounds it. Paint cans litter the yard, but there's no painter anywhere in sight. The old paint hasn't been scraped off. Nothing at all has been done. Satisfied, they drive home.

Shirley and her mother and sisters don't drive by the Mimses' house. Her mother won't go that far. Patty reports that a boy she knows went up and looked in the window, but all he saw was a TV with the Smothers Brothers on. The good part was, the room was pitch dark.

The best rumor of all is that Ginger Ficklin is pregnant with Cal Mims's baby, proof of the orgies Babe and Babe and Babe indulge in. Soon, Ginger Ficklin will produce a half-brother or half-sister for Manda. Shirley, accompanying her mother to the grocery store, hears three different due dates.

In the church lobby hangs a sign-up sheet for the antiwar demonstration in DC, and every Sunday, Shirley checks it for new names. Cal Mims will fill his bus.

With an evil grin, Patty whispers, "Let's sign up Mama and Daddy," but of course they don't do it. Suggested supplies are listed on the church bulletin board: *Food for 2 days, sleeping bag, water, toilet paper.*

"Maybe they're going to camp on the White House lawn," Patty says in a sarcastic TV voice, but their speculation is cut short by the start of the service.

Amid organ music, Cal Mims makes his ponderous way to the pulpit. The pews are so full that Shirley can barely see him. Across the aisle, Ray West sits very quietly in a starched white shirt. His brother David has departed for boot camp. Shirley can't tell how she feels about him. Her love isn't as strong these days. He is growing his hair out. David's had gotten long, past his collar. Will he have to get his head shaved before he goes to Nam?

"Anybody know where I can get a megaphone?" Cal asks. "When we're in DC, we've gotta be heard." He holds a fist toward his mouth. "We're gonna be heard, and we're gonna be seen." His love beads look like M&M's. "Let us pray."

One good thing about Cal Mims: Shirley never cries when he prays, the way she did with the old preacher, whose voice was so rich and reverent that her eyes filled and overflowed no matter how hard she tried to think of funny things. Cal's prayers bump and stumble, and they're folksy, as if he thinks Jesus is some buddy of his, hanging around with time on his hands.

She opens her eyes during the prayer and finds that many other people's eyes are open too. What is everybody waiting for? What are they hoping will happen?

And what does love mean? The more she focuses on the word, the idea, the fuzzier it gets. She loves her family, her cats, ZeeZee, and probably Ray. Her parents and ZeeZee love her back. Even the cats and her sisters love her a little bit. For other people, love must be different.

Someday she will know how all of this turns out. Years from now, she and her mother will look back on the Summer of Love, filtering through the reports that will eventually reach their ears: how the whole season culminated in the bus ride to Washington, DC, where it rained continuously for three days, whereupon Cal Mims, Ginger Ficklin, *Y'all bring your own meat,* and their followers, including Tilma Harrell and her mother, crawled back on the bus and headed to a rock concert for activities so infamous that Cal Mims never again showed his face in Glen Allen, except for a single day, when he and his family packed up and moved to California.

Will he ever say Amen? As he prays on, Shirley senses his days are numbered. The old preacher will be welcomed back with cakes and applause. Shirley glances across the aisle at Ray West. His eyes are open, and he catches her gaze and holds it. Oh, his calm attention, focused all on her, is more exciting than any smile. At last, he blinks and slouches down in the pew, and she looks over at Ginger Ficklin.

Ginger's eyes are open too, and she is beaming up at Cal Mims. She is still slender. There is no sign of a baby, but her pink dress looks crushed and limp, as if it's been through a lot, as if it will fall right off her.

III

THE BEST PARTY EVER

August 1967

"What will you remember about today?" asks Shirley's mother, lying on the brass bed in Diana's room.

It's a question she has asked her daughters many times before. It's one of their pastimes, more than a game. Shirley has turned nine, and she feels a restless envy toward Patty, who sits on the floor and rubs her bare legs with a new grooming aid, a gray mitt covered in fine sandpaper, like a gentle emery board. Shirley roams the room, unwilling to lie down yet unable to leave the pull of the others' company. Diana is stretched out beside their mother.

"What will you remember?" their mother prompts.

"Blackie didn't want to nurse the kittens anymore," Diana says.

"I'll remember finding a dead bumblebee in your sewing basket, Mama," Patty says. "It's pretty. Let's let it stay there."

Patty's mitt creates a funny smell, the odor of hair ground to powder. The mitt is a sign of change. Soon Patty will be shaving her legs. Shirley has employed the mitt on her own skin, but only briefly, because Patty protests she'll use it up. Scouring away leg hair, the mitt makes skin so slick it feels almost numb. Patty gets to experience everything first, and she has a penchant for dramatic encounters. Shirley remembers them all: the time Patty cut her hand on a jagged blue mirror they'd found in the attic; the time she tried to pet a wild tomcat she named Black Rain. She bears the scars of the mirror and of Black Rain's assault.

Patty launches into a tale about two of her friends who were wronged by a teacher. Shirley can't bear the melodrama. It's as bad as the dusty, feety smells created by the mitt, as bad as their mother's dreamy abstraction as she lies on the bed, the late afternoon light catching on the hairs above her lip. Somehow, danger lurks.

Shirley recalls an incident from the previous summer. On a day of murderous heat, her mother drove them back from ZeeZee's house in Richmond. They left the flowery calm of ZeeZee's neighborhood for the business district of Broad Street, a massive channel of traffic running east and west. They headed toward Staples Mill Road, which would take them away from the city and into the country fields and the small farms of Glen Allen.

As Shirley's mother turned a corner, another car careened past, and a man stuck his head out the window and yelled, *Why dincha put your turn light on!* With his red face and streaming gray hair, he was rage personified. All the way home, Shirley's mother said, *I did use my signal. I'm sure I did,* and her face was a wide-open study in hurt. They were all shocked. Patty recovered first, condemning the man so violently that by the time they reached their driveway, their mother managed a weak chuckle. Shirley felt shaken the rest of the day. For anybody to act that way to her mother and get away with it was appalling.

Shirley can generally tell what her mother is going to do. She does use turn lights, in the car and in almost everything she does. She is the most predictable person Shirley knows, a creature of routine and habit. Yet Shirley worries about her. She worries about her father, too, and wishes they would fret more about each other, so she wouldn't have to. When her mother reported the turn-light man, Shirley's father said, *What an awful something he must've been.* His face showed he took in the magnitude of the ordeal, yet Shirley could tell her mother was still upset. There was nothing to be done.

Now Patty's petition to keep the dead bumblebee in the sewing basket goes unchallenged, though Shirley expects that the next time her mother sews, she herself will be called upon to dispose of the furry golden body. Disposing of dead bumblebees is somehow her responsibility, in the same category as making coffee for her parents in the mornings. But she will not throw the bumblebee out. She'll put it in her jewelry box.

It's almost suppertime. A casserole made of ground beef, rice, onions, and tomatoes is ready on the stove downstairs, but Shirley's father is late.

"Probably just a lot of traffic," her mother says, and Shirley knows she is glad for extra time to lie on the bed.

Traffic. Shirley sees again the turn-light man's heatwave hair, his broken veins and mouth of thunder, and his fierce, split-second reaction to her mother's driving: *Why dincha put your turn light on.* She shudders. She had believed that months of shoving the memory away had banished him, but he is still lurking, bursting out. She wishes she had avenged her mother, had shrieked something to humble him.

He is still causing trouble, pushing Shirley to desperation. She has to stop Patty's monologue and break through her mother's preoccupation.

"Mama," she says, "what would you do if something happened to Daddy? Would you get a job?"

"Oh," her mother cries, as if a needle has jabbed her. "Why do you say that, Shirley?"

Patty pauses in mid-rub, holding the gray mitt high above a polished knee, her mouth an O. Her face registers advantage. Diana rolls off the bed, goes to her toy box, and begins a game of jacks.

"Why did you say that, Shirley?" Patty echoes.

"Sometimes I just wonder about it," Shirley mumbles.

This is true, though there's no reason for concern. Her father is healthy, he is only middle-aged, and his career as an engineer with the state Water Control Board seems secure. Shirley simply does not believe her mother could manage a job, if only because it would mean being alert in the morning.

Their present life does not require her mother to leave the house unless she wants to. She goes out only to shop, perform errands, attend church, and visit relatives. No, that's not true. She does a lot more. She takes Shirley and her sisters to the doctor and the dentist, and there are plenty of other tasks that involve going out, and there is little to stop her if she so desires. The ease of a grownup's life never ceases to confound Shirley. Yet there is something childlike about her mother, some refusal to admit to dreadful possibilities, that Shirley finds frustrating. She wants to protect her mother, yet she wants her to be sure and certain in the perilous world.

Her mother's work, Shirley admits, is never-ending. During the school year, Shirley can't bear to watch her wearily packing lunches at night. The lunches are haphazard, like those a child might fix, with an emphasis on sweets—cookies, cupcakes, breakfast pastries. In the morning, the paper bags are cold and soft from a night in the icebox. Lunches aside, Shirley and her sisters' spells of discontent bring to their mother's face a puckered, bewildered expression that Shirley finds haunting. Years later, when she believes herself to be an expert on emotions, she will tell herself that she was only trying to empower her mother. Yet memories will break her heart: she'll recall her mother saying of a book, *I never want it to end,* and she will wonder what book that was, what story was speaking to her mother's educated mind and her tender, word-loving heart.

And her mother has lived deeply, enormously. Her tales of World War Two, the recollections of a Richmond teenager, will always be as real to Shirley as the skin on her own hands: how she worked weekends at a telegraph office and took off her shoes after work, late at night, and ran home barefoot because she was scared and could move faster in bare feet; how her father, a doctor, was sick during the war, ill from a stroke and in bed all day, a massive, stern man driven to helpless tears by his condition, knowing he would die and leave his family poor; how restaurants served cream cheese instead of butter. Shirley doesn't understand how cream cheese could have been a deprivation. But the sick, weeping father and the dashing through dark streets—these things are terrifying. "I used to think up ways for people to say things in fewer words," her mother has said of the telegraph office, "so they could save money." She has told of the time her father collapsed at the bottom of the steps and how her mother, tiny ZeeZee, in a rush of adrenaline gathered the huge man in her arms and carried him up the stairs: "She did it because she had to." Shirley has practiced on heavy objects, attempting to lift a sofa—*Ray West*—and failing, though she tells herself: *Pick it up, or Ray will die.*

She should never have asked her mother such an unspeakable question: *What if something happened to Daddy?* The air is sharp with her mother's indignation and Patty's delight. Patty is the better daughter. She has started rolling up her hair at night like their mother does. The wheels of hair, skewered with bobby pins, give them a wizardly look.

Yes, Patty is a miniature of their mother, though her theatrics and talkativeness are her own. Diana is always playing dreamy little games as if inhabiting a world of fairies. What is left for Shirley? She doesn't want to be just like them. Her role is that of the watcher, the light sleeper, on guard against harm. She has to shield them, especially her mother, and she fails every time. Instead of getting rid of their anxiety, she makes it worse.

Her mother sighs and eases off the bed, her face puffy. Even her feet, scuffing for her sandals, sound unhappy. Shirley's heart is heavy with grief. Time and again, she'll hurt the ones she loves, will thrust their frailties in their faces, and she'll be as she is now, dry-throated and full of remorse.

Thank goodness, there's the gravelly crunch of her father's car in the driveway. He's safe. He'll burst through the door, cheerful and smelling of the city.

✦ ✦ ✦

SHIRLEY has a new worry. Her mother doesn't want to go anywhere. In the morning, her father leaves for work as he always does, and then she and her sisters spend their day in summer pursuits. There is the rope swing that hangs from an elm tree, glorious for sailing wide and high, with the danger of falling off the knotted rope or smacking into the great trunk when you return. There are the cats to play with, bricks to overturn and search beneath for spiders, flowers to gather and arrange, books to read, games to play—Parcheesi, Monopoly, and Old Maid. Brownies can be baked, though it's hard not to burn the chocolate when you melt it. Their mother fixes lunch: sandwiches and Pepsi to be consumed in front of the TV, with soap operas playing out their romances, which seem to Shirley increasingly stale and silly.

There are vegetables to be picked in the garden, and the weather in all its charm, hot days full of buzzing honeybees, cool shadows under the maple trees beside the porch, and wet spells when the pelting rain makes Shirley think of marching soldiers. In late afternoon, her favorite time of day, birds make sounds like thoughtful conversation interspersed with song, and her mother is busy in the kitchen, fixing supper.

All of this is lovely, except they never go anywhere. Her mother never wants to leave the property, if she has to drive. On weekends, Shirley's father takes them to visit ZeeZee, and they stop for ice cream at High's. As they pass a grocery store, Shirley's mother will say, "Let me run in and get a few things."

With Shirley's father at the wheel, they go to Overhill Lake and spend all day swimming, drying off, swimming some more, and getting wonderful hot dogs at the snack bar. Even better, sometimes they go to the beach, usually Yorktown or Buckroe. One Saturday, they go to the wilder, rougher Virginia Beach, where Patty is caught in surf at the very edge of the sand and is rolled dramatically. Shirley's father plucks Patty from the waves, but the episode causes Shirley's mother to slowly grow hysterical and to insist they go home at once. Patty sleeps in the front seat the whole way, her head in their mother's lap.

Patty's friends are all turning twelve. Patty attends Evie Cartwright's birthday party because it's on a Saturday, and her father can drive her. She reports that Evie's cake came from a bakery. Of all Patty's friends, the most sophisticated are Evie and a girl named Linda.

They wear two-piece bathing suits at Overhill Lake. They have not only started their periods, they are using tampons, a fact Patty generously shares with Shirley.

"Guess what," Patty says. "A tampon fell out of Linda's pocketbook, and boys saw it, but they didn't know what it was, so they didn't say anything."

Shirley knows when to just listen.

"Linda says it's an old wives' tale that you can't bathe during your period," Patty says. "Mama only takes sponge baths then. Did you know that? I'm going to bathe."

Shirley could ask her mother about all of this, but it's more fun to find out from Patty, who is up to date.

So there are outings on weekends, but during the week, her mother says to Shirley and her sisters, "Let's just stay here today."

There are long naps, with her mother and sisters stretched out on Diana's brass bed, while Shirley wanders outside, desultorily climbing trees. Sometimes there are two or three naps a day. She decides to wait it out.

"Can't we go somewhere, Mama?" Diana finally says. "To the pool?"

"It's too hot to go anywhere," their mother says, but concedes that a dip would feel good.

She drags a blue plastic wading pool from a shed, and she and Patty and Shirley and Diana take turns blowing into it to inflate the sides. The puffing makes Shirley dizzy. Sunshine and clover spin when she opens her eyes, and the mildewy plastic scalds her throat. Shirley's mother turns on the hose. A few inches of cold, earthy-smelling water gather in the soft bottom.

"Put your suits on," their mother says, and they do, though Patty says this is babyfied; she wants a real pool. Their mother puts on her bathing suit too, and lowers herself slowly into the water, saying, "Oh. Oh."

She smooths out the bottom, worrying aloud that weeds might puncture the plastic. The water barely covers their laps. The shoulder straps of Shirley's nylon bathing suit, an old one of Patty's, feel tight. Shirley, her sisters, and their mother can barely fit into the pool together. They hug their knees to their chests.

Shirley senses disaster at hand when Diana grabs Leopold, the tomcat, and plops him into the pool. He strikes out, ripping a long tear. All the water seeps out. Leopold's wet fur leaves a sharp yellow reek as he bounds away.

"We still have the hose," her mother offers. "We can spray each other."

And there is an old hand pump in a field where the water is icy even in hottest summer, smelling of iron. They could splash themselves at that pump. But these ideas are discarded, and her mother decides on a nap instead.

Shirley and her sisters drag the ruined pool to the clothesline and pin it up to dry. Maybe their father can patch the torn place. Shirley yearns for the turquoise water of Overhill Lake, the chlorine in her nose, the hot dogs and slatted floor of the snack bar, and the company of others, lifeguards blowing whistles, teenagers shouting wise, exotic remarks. Patty and Diana slip away, leaving Shirley in the yard. She wanders over to the driveway, to the family's second car, an aging gray Plymouth which has not been driven in so long that weeds are sprouting around its tires. A few cats follow.

Maybe if she gets in the car, that will make her mother want to come out and go somewhere. She opens the door on the driver's side, and hot musty air pours out. The cats stay back. She leans in to examine the steering wheel and the pedals, the heat tightening around her head. The car feels as foreign as a spaceship. The dashboard holds as much dust as the floor beneath her bed. She sits down behind the wheel, but the seat is scorching. She jumps out, and the turn-light man leaps into her brain, his presence as powerful as if he'd goosed her. She slams the door.

There is nothing whatsoever to do.

She can't wait to grow up and drive. Yes, someday she can drive to Overhill Lake by herself the way teenagers do, their faces proud and smug behind dark sunglasses. Does that life await her? She hopes so. She tries to picture herself grown, with a husband and children. How would that be? She can't imagine. She wants to be here always, in this place of cats and tall trees, yet she wants the pool and driving, too.

She senses her mother is recovering from some long spell of hardship, keeping up with meals and laundry, but it's as if these chores are harder than usual for her. Shirley remembers the look on her face on the winter day she was diagnosed with pneumonia and sent to the hospital—a haunted, mortal expression. This must be some continuation of her resting, getting back to the thoughts she was having before the illness and the hospital. It's as if she's gathering her strength in readiness for all the crooked teeth and outgrown clothes she'll have to face. Three times she will cope with first periods. She will treat a thousand colds. It is cumulative exhaustion she feels, a crushing sense of responsibility. Her answer is this retreat—naps, potato chips, and daytime TV, abstraction as she empties trash cans, irons clothes, and rinses glasses at the sink.

"Are you all right, Mama?" Shirley asks one day when they are alone. Patty and Diana are outside feeding the cats.

"I'm fine," her mother says. A struggle passes over her face. "Oh, I ought to lose weight and get a job."

"Has Daddy said that?"

"No, but Mother says I've put on weight. All the magazines say you should get a job, plus be perfect at home. They say, now it's the sixties, and life is different."

Shirley reads the magazines too, *McCall's* and *Ladies' Home Journal*. One advertisement shows a distraught woman gripping a bedpost. The ad mentions odor, and the caption says, *There are some problems a married woman faces alone.* The product being sold is a white capsule. Is it some kind of medicine or soap? Does the woman or her husband smell bad, or something in the room? Month after month, the woman remains unenlightened. By now, she might have ripped that post right off the bed.

Jackie Kennedy, the most frequent guest in the magazines, never looks uncertain or flat-out desperate, like the bedpost woman, even though the magazines talk about how alone she is. Jackie Kennedy gets all the sympathy and all the admiration, and she probably doesn't spend one second holding a bedpost.

Shirley's mother regards her beseechingly.

"Just read *My Weekly Reader*," Shirley advises.

The latest issue features a Turkish boy who is ambidextrous. "Both-Handed Bedri" the headline says. He has sparked considerable discussion within the family, and Shirley's mother has avowed that Both-Handed Bedri is a lot more fun than Jackie Kennedy.

"Magazines are too expensive, anyway," she says, "and I shouldn't be worrying, since it's summertime. Oh, Shirley, I guess I'm depressed. Do you know how that feels?"

"Yes." Shirley is struck to the heart by the open book of her mother's face.

"How could you know? You're too little to be depressed."

"I just know."

Shirley is depressed about a lot of things, when she stops to think about them, but she won't tell her mother about that. The newspaper, after all, is full of war. "Ho's Shoes Would Be Hard to Fill" is the title of an editorial. Ho, she understands, is Ho Chi Minh, and he is a communist. Chills race through her, as if the shoes of the fierce stranger are guns pointed at her head.

One day, Diana says to Patty and Shirley, "We never go anywhere. What's wrong with Mama?"

"Nothing," Patty says. She is their mother's defender, but her brow is furrowed. "It would be nice to go to a store or something. Or a movie, or the library."

"We haven't even been to ZeeZee's in a long time," Diana points out.

"I need to see my friends," Patty declares.

"Let's go find Mama," Shirley says. She pours Pepsi into a glass. They locate their mother on the front porch swing, sitting quietly, not rocking.

"Tell us about the girl who fixed stockings," Shirley says.

This is a story from World War Two. Their mother sips the Pepsi.

"She was a year older than I was," she says, "and good at sewing. Stockings were hard to get. You could hardly ever buy new ones."

"Get to the good part," Diana prompts.

"She used to hold them up to the light, to see how bad the holes were." Their mother lifts invisible stockings. "If she didn't like somebody, even if the runs weren't bad, she'd say, 'I'm sorry, I can't fix this for you.'" She laughs.

Shirley wants to think up a new question. That will please her.

"How did she learn how to fix them? And how much did she charge?"

"Not very much. I think she used her own hair for thread. Oh, that war," her mother says. "It lasted so long, and you didn't know when it would be over."

The phone rings, and Patty runs to answer it. Their mother yawns and says to Shirley and Diana, "I think I'll lie down for a while. Will you-all be all right? You could rest with me."

Patty returns, excited. "That was Linda. She's having a party, right now. Can I go?"

Their mother sighs. "You just went to Evie Cartwright's party."

"That was ages ago. And Linda just got Incredible Edibles. She said I can use it."

Shirley knows what this treasure is. It involves the use of flavored gum that can be baked, with a clever machine, into the shapes of insects.

Patty digs in her heels. "I'm tired of always being here."

"It's a bad idea to drop everything and run over, every time somebody calls," their mother says. "Besides, I'd have to drive you, and I'm tired. Can Linda's mother come get you?"

"Her mother's busy," says Patty. "She's making a new type of fudge. It's got Velveeta cheese in it."

"That sounds horrible," their mother says.

"Linda says it's good!"

Shirley gulps, startled by the escalation of this argument. She hopes Patty won't give up. Someday she might be in Patty's place.

Shirley longs to go, too. Imagine—a party that started just because popular Linda picked up the phone.

"It doesn't sound like a real party," their mother says. "People just hanging around somebody's house can be a nuisance."

"But she said to come right over," Patty says.

"She should have called earlier," their mother says. "This looks like you were forgotten, or passed over when invitations were sent out."

"You're making this too hard." Patty bursts into tears. "I'm going to tell everybody you never leave the house."

She runs to her room and sets up a chorus of sobs.

Shirley is scared. More than Incredible Edibles is at stake. Their mother retreats to Diana's room, lies down on the brass bed, and covers her face with her hands. Patty's cries bounce off the walls: wails and tremolos, barks and keening. It goes on and on. The day grows hotter. Outside, the mockingbirds fall silent.

"I can't stand it," their mother says.

She rises from the bed and heads for Patty's room. In the hallway, Shirley and Diana raise fearful eyes to each other and listen to the sharp exchange that follows. Patty and their mother have never before raised their voices at each other. They are two grownups fighting.

Finally, their mother emerges, her face white and embattled.

"Get in the car," she says.

Patty is behind her with a remote expression and swollen eyes. She descends the stairs with dignity, and Shirley and Diana scramble to follow.

The time of day is wrong for going downtown, the air seething and evil. It's rush hour, the very time of day the turn-light man struck. He is so palpable he might be sitting in the car with them, all streaming hair and raging mouth. Shirley shivers through her sweat. Patty sits ramrod-straight beside their mother, with Shirley and Diana in the back. Nobody speaks. Their mother drives fast, taking turns crisply and speeding through yellow lights. The car hums with her anger. Hot wind boils through the windows and snarls their hair across their faces.

In minutes, they reach ZeeZee's neighborhood, with its familiar brick townhouses and pots of petunias. ZeeZee is out on her shady front porch, on her glider, reading a magazine. She stands up in surprise when she sees their car.

Shirley's mother doesn't even park. She calls out from the car window, "Shirley and Diana are going to visit you for a while. Patty and I have something to do."

"All right, Daughter," ZeeZee says, picking up on the air of urgency and discord, addressing her in the old-fashioned way.

Shirley and Diana tumble out of the car, and it lurches off.

ZeeZee ushers them into her house, which has its summer decor of white rugs and floor fans. Shirley feels instant relief from the heat and tension. Because ZeeZee keeps her shades drawn on hot days, the house stays as cool as if it were air-conditioned. She stirs up a pitcher of lemonade and finds cookies in the pantry. Shirley and Diana play tag in the backyard.

"I don't know how you-all can play out here in this heat," ZeeZee observes, but she doesn't stop them.

There is time for a nap, and Shirley and Diana stick together, choosing the blue room that was their mother's. For once, Shirley is sleepy in the afternoon, but she wakes when the phone rings. ZeeZee keeps her voice low: "Everything's fine. Shirley and Diana are here. Jean said there was something she and Patty had to do," and Shirley knows her father is on the phone, it is late enough that he got home and found them gone. Even in her drowsiness, she senses the worry he must have felt.

It gets so late that ZeeZee fixes supper.

"Yay, fried chicken," says Diana, as she and Shirley enter the kitchen.

ZeeZee is mixing cake batter, too. Shirley hopes she and Diana can spend the night. But the front door opens, and here come Patty and their mother, Patty toting a bag from Miller & Rhoads and exuding the store's floral, sparkling fragrance.

"We were there till they closed," Patty says. "They had to unlock a special door for us."

"What did you get?" ZeeZee cries, dusting her hands on her apron.

Patty reaches into the bag and lifts out a white garment with elastic and lace. "Bras."

"Well, training bras," their mother says. She looks exhausted but calm. Something has passed.

They stay for supper, though Patty says casually, for Shirley and Diana's benefit, "I'm not really hungry. We had a snack at the Tea Room."

ZeeZee gives Shirley the fried chicken liver, knowing she loves it. ZeeZee and Diana pull the wishbone. Patty goes to put on one of her new bras, but she refuses to let anybody see her in it except ZeeZee, who raves over how pretty she looks.

Patty reappears. "Can you see it through my blouse?" she asks, hoping.

Their mother tells ZeeZee, "The clerk said to wear a beige bra under white clothes. Beige doesn't show under white. I didn't know that."

"You didn't, Daughter?" ZeeZee says.

"Well, we ought to be going home," Shirley's mother says.

ZeeZee wraps fried chicken and cake in waxed paper. "Here, Daughter, for Merle."

✦   ✦   ✦

PATTY is turning twelve. For this milestone, she's having a party, and not just a regular birthday party, but one with a theme: beauty parlor. Girls only, "a hen party," their mother says. Evie Cartwright promises to bring her older sister's lighted makeup mirror. Linda offers her mother's hood-style hair dryer.

"Ask her to make Velveeta fudge," Shirley tells Patty, and is rewarded with a frown. Patty is not to be teased these days.

"What about curling irons?" ZeeZee suggests, their routine visits with her having been reestablished. ZeeZee twirls a lock of Patty's thick brown hair and says, "I could do your whole head in about ten minutes. Candle-style curls."

This threat of being carried back to the nineteenth century puts the familiar frown on Patty's face again. Shirley can actually see a line there, right between her eyebrows.

Patty's major disappointment is that the gathering will not be a slumber party. Their mother refuses to have ten girls as overnight guests. Patty pleads: sleeping bags could be borrowed, and Shirley and Diana wouldn't mind giving up their beds for one night, would they? Some of the girls could sleep on the sofa. This has been done at other houses.

"No, they're all going home by five o'clock," their mother says.

At the supper table, Patty says, "I wish we had a shower instead of that old tub. This house is so old-fashioned."

"Take everybody out to the pump," their father says, and to Shirley, this is a good idea.

"Think how *that* would look," Patty says. "I'll tell everybody to come with their hair already washed."

"I hope they will," their mother says. "Who'd go to a party with dirty hair?"

Shirley and Diana laugh, but Patty jumps up and leaves the room.

"To think Patty will be in junior high this fall," their mother says. "You-all are growing up so fast."

When Shirley and Diana clear the table, Diana pauses, plate in hand, a dolphin-like smile on her lips.

"Make sure to get mints for the party, Mama," she says.

"I will," their mother promises.

"Patty wants to get her ears pierced," Shirley volunteers, eager to get Patty in trouble.

Their mother's jaw drops. "Absolutely not. Are other girls having that done?"

"They're doing each other's, with needles and ice cubes," Shirley can't resist telling, though she knows of only two girls who did this, and they aren't among the party guests. She has glimpsed the needled, ice-cubed ears, and has to admit the handiwork isn't bad.

"Needles and ice cubes," her mother gasps.

The party is in trouble, even in danger of being canceled, until Patty is confronted and asked for assurance that no such thing will take place under the Lloyds' roof.

"None of my friends would do *that*," Patty fumes. "Linda had her ears pierced by a doctor. Do you think *Linda* would use *a needle* and an *ice cube?*" Another storm is in the offing, as her eyes brim with righteous tears.

What this is really about, Shirley knows, is boys. Curls and pierced ears are all about boys. Apparently, people aren't much different from cats, old Leopold the tomcat biting a female's neck and climbing on her back. Hair spray and makeup and years of phone calls between girls, that's what lies ahead for Patty and her friends and presumably for Shirley and Diana too, while they wait for a boy to ask them out, and once one of them does, then what? Shirley can't imagine what you'd say to a boy for a whole date. Her conversations with boys are limited to one-liners. Even with Ray West, what would she say? It would only take a few seconds to tell him what happened to his lunch box, and he might not even care.

Patty's birthday arrives at last, "so breathlessly hot," their mother says, spreading seven-minute frosting on a big chocolate cake, "look, the top layer is sliding off."

She never uses cake mixes or canned icing. Those are the hallmarks of laziness, public admissions of incompetence. *You can always tell a mix*, she says, indicating, without ever saying so, that people who use them are playing a trick on husband, children, partygoers, bake sale customers, church supper guests. Mixes are cheap shortcuts, con artists' ploys, the chemical aftertaste giving away the secret, like Betty Crocker showing her underpants. If you're going to have something as marvelous as a cake, why substitute a mix? Yet these days, mixes are *ubiquitous*—a favorite word of Shirley's mother's.

Patty panics about the sliding-apart cake.

"I'll use toothpicks to hold it together," their mother says, "and I'll put it in the icebox."

Shirley feels worried. She has seen a toothpicked cake tear itself apart on a hot day, whole chunks bursting, slumping, and caving in.

Patty keeps on about the cake. "You ought not to ice it so soon, Mama. You just took it out of the oven. And don't say *icebox*. Nobody says that anymore. Say *refrigerator*."

Only because it's her birthday does Patty get away with such criticism. Their mother asks Patty and Shirley to set the table. There are matching pink plates and napkins, and pink-and-white balloons that are almost as hard to blow up as the wading pool. That episode seems long ago. Diana is enlisted, and at last all of the balloons are inflated and tied in a cascade of paper ribbons to the brass chandelier above the table, to splendid effect. Behind Patty's back, Diana opens her hand and reveals to Shirley a clutch of mints, smudges of wet pastel in her palm, and they know better than to show Patty.

Next, they put a favor at each guest's place, a roll of LifeSavers taped to a packet of flower seeds.

"I hope they'll actually plant these, not let them go to waste," their mother says. "Maybe we should save the seeds and just give the Life-Savers. This got right expensive."

Shirley and Diana begin to separate the seed packets from the Life-Savers, but Patty objects, "I don't want to look like a cheapskate."

The seed packets are reinstated, with much discussion as to who should receive zinnias, cosmos, portulacas, or marigolds. Should there be place cards?

"Wherever they happen to sit, that's what they get," their mother says in a voice that brooks no further argument, "and we're not going to let them get all balled up with trading, either. This is the last time I'll do all this with seeds."

What to wear? Shirley and Diana can stay in shorts, their mother says. Patty wants to dress up. She runs upstairs and returns to the kitchen in the dress she wore on Chorus Day, her face anguished. The dress is too small, tight at the armholes and riding high above her knees.

"Well, you can wear shorts, too," their mother says, but Patty refuses. It's her party, her day, and she needs something special. And the way things are going—her lip trembles—with the cake sliding apart, and her dress too little, and, and . . .

Lounging at the kitchen door, Diana says, "Look!"

A little snub-nosed van has pulled up in the driveway, emblazoned with the ribbon-and-bow trademark of Miller & Rhoads. A delivery man hops out with a package in his hand. Patty, Shirley, and Diana rush outside.

"For Miss Patricia Lloyd," the man says.

Patty takes the package and runs back inside, with Shirley and Diana following.

Their mother sets down the icing-covered spatula, smiling. "I bet I know who sent it."

Patty tears the box open. It's a dress from ZeeZee, and it's so much better than the ruffly Chorus Day outfit, which by contrast looks silly and childish. All of their clothes—Patty's and Shirley's and Diana's and their mother's—are shown to be outmoded and contemptible by the existence of this sleeveless linen sheath. It's lined with silk, and in the bodice are actual darts, so Patty's training bra will not be wasted. It is dark green, the most sophisticated garment ever to come into the house.

Patty hugs it. "It's gorgeous," she says, and is off to call ZeeZee, whose status at the moment equals that of Linda and Evie.

Somehow, ZeeZee always knows their sizes. She used to work at Miller & Rhoads herself, as a clerk in the girls' department. She has to watch every penny, just as the Lloyds do. Yet the presents from her are always wonderful. She might not know that curling irons haven't been used in a hundred years, but she knows clothes. She can sew, too. She uses Vogue patterns to make stylish suits cut from soft wool, and flowered cotton dresses for summertime. She knows what girls turning twelve will love. She is still a teenager herself, though she's old and all of her friends have diverticulitis. Shirley imagines ZeeZee going up the escalator at Miller & Rhoads, heading deep into the hallowed territory of the third floor, to the girls' department, and finding a clerk who remembers her, the two of them greeting each other with the high, raving enthusiasm of females about to engage in a pleasant transaction. With unerring instinct, ZeeZee picked out the prettiest dress on the rack.

"Is ZeeZee coming to the party?" Shirley asks.

Her mother's hands, icing the cake, freeze in midair. "I didn't even think to ask her. This is a party for Patty's friends."

"What if she wants to come?" Shirley persists.

Oh, Shirley is merciless, a needle and an ice cube both, and her mother should throw her out of the house. Shirley decides she'll never have children. She doesn't want any short, wiry critics underfoot.

"We'll go visit her tomorrow," her mother says, "so she can see Patty in the dress."

Outside, the sky is a sizzling blue. Down in the garden, the roses Patty was counting on for a centerpiece have wilted. Diana, dispatched to locate substitute flowers, returns with a drooping handful of Queen Anne's lace, trumpet vine, and chicory. It's a bunch of weeds, but Shirley won't say so. Her mother will arrange these lowly blossoms in a vase and slip a doily beneath, and it will be beautiful.

In the heat and steam of the kitchen, the icing is developing a problem of its own, the airy egg-white fluff melting into a glaze.

"I didn't wait for the cake to cool enough," her mother admits.

Shirley doesn't dare ask about the strawberry ice cream. The tiny freezer in the icebox—*refrigerator*, she reminds herself—never keeps food frozen for long, though it has a habit of developing vicious icicles, like teeth, that require her mother to defrost it frequently. Ice cream goes soft as cottage cheese in the little compartment, but the metal ice trays within it manage to create slick cubes. Shirley takes out an ice tray and yanks back the metal rod, and the frosty metal burns her hands. She puts ice cubes in a glass, fills it with water, and hands it to her mother, who drinks deeply.

"The cake will still taste good," Shirley says.

Her mother nods, holding the glass to her hot face.

"The party will go by as fast as a dream," she says. "Someday we'll look back on this day and remember it."

They know that amid the pink hurrah of the party, Patty will be too distracted to spurn the renegade cake.

Patty twirls into the kitchen in her new dress. She is made for sororities, for circles of intimates and confidantes. Never has anyone been so ready for seventh grade. She will navigate cliques and breeze among warring knots of junior women, forming blood ties of loyalty and remembrance among girls as stubborn and hopeful as she is, as innocent and determined as she will always be. She will live a life as harbored and protected as a dove in a nest, ever vocal, ever on the phone, a scorner of cake mixes, a champion of the birthdays of those she loves, a shedder of complicated tears, winsome as ZeeZee, and like ZeeZee, happiest as a hostess and skilled in homing in on fashions for younger generations, right on target when choosing a dress that will make a granddaughter seize it from its box, the folded tissue paper whispering to the floor.

"You have other presents, Patty," their mother says, pointing to a stack of wrapped bundles. Shirley knows what is inside each one.

"I could wait to open them at the party," Patty says.

"No," Shirley and Diana say together. Shirley is incensed: Patty is trying to act like a grownup.

"Well, then I'd have a bigger pile," Patty explains.

"You ought not to open presents from your family in front of guests," their mother says. Her rules of etiquette are not questioned. "It's private. That means you either open them now or wait till the party's over."

Patty doesn't wait. She unwraps a troll from Shirley, one they have traded back and forth and which is a special favorite of Patty's, with its fizz of orange hair; Silly Putty from Diana, slightly dirty because Diana has played with it, a fact Patty is kind enough not to mention; and the prize—a leather pocketbook from their mother, with a matching wallet inside. Patty groups and regroups the presents. She praises the troll and puts it on Shirley's shoulder.

"We still have to eat lunch," their mother says, "even if it is a party day."

She fixes egg salad sandwiches and slices some fresh peaches. After Shirley finishes her peach, her fingertips burn like they did on the metal ice tray, and her lips and tongue itch. Red spots break out on her arms. It can't be measles. She's had measles already.

"I feel funny, Mama. Look at my arms."

"It's hives," her mother says. "You're allergic to something. I bet it was that peach."

"Linda's allergic to cats," Patty puts in.

"It's not the cats," Shirley protests.

Her mother is always saying there are too many. That would be awful, to hand her an excuse to banish them. Shirley's skin prickles, and her lips swell. She claws at her face and arms.

"I'll give you some Benadryl," her mother says, "but it'll make you sleepy."

A spoonful of the red liquid eases the itchiness right away. Shirley's mother and Patty and Diana go into high gear, turning Patty's room into a beauty salon.

"I bought this," their mother says, and produces a jar of green fluid. "Setting lotion. You dip your comb in it before you roll up your hair. It makes curls last longer."

A card table, covered with an embroidered dresser scarf, will hold the makeup mirror. The hair dryer will be in Diana's room, which has an extra electrical socket.

Diana is thrilled. "They can borrow my brush," she says, and this creates minor panic.

"Don't ever share your brush," their mother says. "You could pick up some disease," to which Patty replies, "Linda and Evie and I use each other's all the time."

"Well, from now on, don't," their mother says in a sharp tone that threatens to ruin the party before it even starts, but somehow Patty stays on an even keel—Shirley thinks of the party as a boat that is navigating ocean waters, threatening to sink—an even keel, which is not Patty's forte.

Shirley feels slow and drowsy, and she's in the way as the others arrange things the guests might want—magazines to read while their curls are being set, talcum powder, and lipstick and nail polish that Patty digs out of their mother's dresser drawers.

"This is just for today," their mother warns. "You're too young to wear makeup for real."

"I know," says Patty mildly.

Shirley knows she owns a tiny lipstick and a compact, wonderful favors given out at Evie Cartwright's party. Seeds can't compare. But Shirley recalls from Patty's reports that Evie's guests just watched her father assemble a barbecue grill. Patty's party, with its ingenious theme, will be much better.

Shirley tries to keep up with her mother and sisters, but it's so hot, and the Benadryl is potent. Sleep tugs at her.

As the first cars pull up in the driveway, she heads for her room, an animal seeking its burrow. Her bed is beside an open window. Gravel crunches steadily as more cars arrive and drive away, mothers dropping off daughters. Excited voices travel through the front hallway. She makes out Evie's and Linda's, and Patty's raised in glee. Perfume wafts upstairs. It's almost as if Patty's guests are their mother's age, they are so grown up, with their scents and loud talk.

In a minute, Shirley will get up and join them. She has waited as long as Patty for this party, but she is between sleep and dozing, and she can't move. They must be getting ready to have the cake and ice cream. That is the plan: they'll eat, then have the beauty salon.

Yes, there's the birthday song, the voices of ten female guests plus Shirley's mother and Diana, lifted beautifully, the tones as exalted as those of a hymn. This means her mother is entering the room grandly, slowly, bearing the lighted cake, setting it down in front of Patty, and standing back as the singing reaches a crescendo. The song fills Patty's ears, surrounding her. Now she's being urged to make a wish. She's closing her eyes and drawing a deep breath, her brain whirring. What is she wishing for? Now she is pursing her lips and blowing out, moving her head back and forth, sending flames spurting sideways until every light turns to smoke.

Applause, lengthy and loud. Next, a flurry of exclamations as the cake is cut and served amid the waxy perfume of candle smoke, and at last, the busy, intimate hush of eating.

✦　✦　✦

SHIRLEY wakes to darkness. Rain falls on the maples in the front yard, the trees closest to her room, pattering through leaves. The washed-linen smell flows through her open window, the first cool breeze in weeks. Her curtains gust out and press against her face. Windows are being closed all over the house, *chump, chump*; she can tell Diana's from Patty's. Is it nighttime? No, late afternoon, says the clock in her head. She holds up her arms, but it's too dim to see if the spots are gone. She knows they are, though. The itching has stopped, and she feels deeply rested.

She gets out of bed, leaving the window up. Her room faces north. Rain won't come in this way, only mist.

In the hallway, she finds Diana, all in shadow.

"You missed the party," Diana says.

"I was asleep."

The sleep was something that was meant to happen, something all her own. The fact that the party went on without her is not the disappointment she might have expected.

"Look," Diana says. Her hair is styled in elaborate ringlets. "Patty's friends did it." Shirley touches the curls. They're as stiff as nylon net. "We ran out of hair spray," Diana says, "and Linda said to use starch. Mama let us have the whole can. Patty got lots of presents. Records and sunglasses and a necklace."

Patty steps out of her room and joins them. She has taken off the green dress and is wearing shorts and a sleeveless blouse that used to belong to their mother, and she is barefoot. In the dimness, she looks so much like their mother that Shirley blinks. The tops of Patty's arms look full and womanly. Her dark hair is arranged in their mother's style, a smooth pageboy.

"They've all gone home," she says. "It was the best party I'll ever have."

The party was not only Patty's triumph, but their mother's too. For their mother and her cake, girls held their breath.

"Is there any cake left?" Shirley says.

"Mama saved you a piece," Diana says.

"Where is she?"

"She's lying down," Patty says. "Let's watch the rain."

170

They all go downstairs and out to the side porch, where cats huddle. The cool air feels glorious. Rain falls hard, flowing out of gutters and onto the concrete patio that must have been created by the Mannings. *Oh, up and down the stairs, Mrs. Manning, up and down the stairs!* Rain gushes and hammers the house and the trees. Shirley runs out into it.

"You'll get wet," Patty cries, but that's the idea.

In an instant, Shirley's shirt and shorts are soaked and clinging to her skin. Diana disappears into the house and returns with her sand pail. She fills it at the gutter spout and offers it to Shirley, who pours the water on her own head, refills the pail, and drenches Diana's ringlets. The curls vanish, leaving Diana's long hair flat. This is even better than the swimming pool. It's raining so hard they don't need the bucket. Shirley tosses it aside and tilts her head. There is no thunder or lightning, just pure rain, tasting like celery.

"Come on, Patty," Diana calls.

"Oh," says Patty, wavering.

She stands at the edge of the porch and sticks one foot out. Their mother appears. She and Patty deliberate. Already their conferences have an air of history and experience. Shirley sees years of such discussions ahead, Patty seeking their mother's advice for everything, their alliance stronger than any that Patty will have with anyone else, even the husband and children who await her in the future.

Their mother has something in her hands, a bottle of shampoo. Patty talks on and on, knowing the art of keeping her listening. It's their mother who moves first, hopping off the porch so lightly she might be Diana's age. She stretches her arms over her head.

In seconds, her dress and apron are sopping wet. She uncaps the bottle of shampoo and pours some onto her hair. Shirley has never seen her behave this way. It's not like Tilma Harrell's mother, it's wonderful. Shirley reaches for the shampoo bottle, and soon she and Diana and their mother are all lather-haired, chasing each other through puddles, slinging wild handfuls of suds, and rinsing themselves by standing straight up, faces to the sky.

Patty tiptoes off the porch in rapid chickeny steps, yelling, "It's cold!"

Acknowledgments

I am happily indebted to the editors of publications where these stories first appeared—Michael Griffith of *The Cincinnati Review*, Michael Koch of *Epoch,* Andrew Scott of *Freight Stories*, Kelly Abbott of *Great Jones Street*, Paula Deitz and Ron Koury of *The Hudson Review*, Marc Smirnoff of *Oxford American*, Carlin Romano and Johnny Temple of *Philadelphia Noir*, and Rod Smith of *Shenandoah*—and to Michael Parker, who judged my work worthy of *Shenandoah*'s Goodheart Prize.

I am grateful to Gillian Berchowitz and the staff at Ohio University Press, including Nancy Basmajian, Sebastian Biot, Jeff Kallet, John Morris, Beth Pratt, Samara Rafert, and Sally Welch, for the diligence and creativity they bestowed on this book; my agent, Liz Darhansoff of Darhansoff & Verrill Literary Agency, and Michele Mortimer of the agency, for their acumen and encouragement; Katie Anderton, for proofreading assistance; the University of Memphis; and the National Endowment for the Arts.

My college sorority, Chi Omega, inspired a portion of this work and deserves tribute for promoting lifelong friendships.

To my sisters, Julia Holladay Mann and Hilary White Holladay, and my husband, John Bensko: my love, affection, and respect.